JOHNNY NEXT DOOR

Some other titles in this series:

THE BLACK PIRATE	JAMES CAHILL
THE FAR-FARERS	CHRIS SAVERY
THE SECRET OF WOODSIDE COTTAGE	L. V. DAVIDSON
PETER JOINS IN	L. V. DAVIDSON
TO THE CITY OF GOLD	CONSTANCE SAVERY
WHITE DEER'S TREASURE	ALFRED J. GILLIARD
FRIENDS FOR JOANNA	ELIZABETH BATT
THE GOLDEN CAP	CONSTANCE SAVERY

The kitten clung to Johnny and began to purr.

JOHNNY NEXT DOOR

N. W. HANSSEN

LUTTERWORTH PRESS
LONDON

First published 1960

Second impression 1966

PRINTED IN GREAT BRITAIN
PHOTOLITHO BY EBENEZER BAYLIS AND SON, LIMITED
THE TRINITY PRESS, WORCESTER, AND LONDON

CONTENTS

Chapter 1

NEW NEIGHBOURS

BY the time that old Mrs. Green died, Johnny next door was well on the way to juvenile delinquency—not that he would have understood the term; he was more used to hearing himself called, "that young demon of Connell's". To do him justice, poor lad, it was scarcely his fault. Almost as far back as he could remember, family life for him was a constant fight between Mum and Dad in which he, an unwilling but fascinated spectator, not infrequently received blows not intended for him. Now that Mum, in a last fit of temper, had run away from home, Dad, wounded in his tenderest vanity both as man and as husband, had taken to drink in good earnest. Meanwhile Mrs. Green, who hated boys in general and Johnny in particular, lost no chance of screaming abuse over the garden fence.

But now Mrs. Green was dead and Johnny, leaning on his gate one sunny afternoon in early June, guessed by the sound of a hammer in the front room next door that someone else had moved in and idly wondered whether the new neighbour was as bad as the old. He turned and looked in at the open window and saw a small, plump, black-haired woman on her knees tacking down a carpet. Johnny shifted a little, trying to see more, and the woman looked up. She saw two deep blue, dark-lashed eyes set in a face that was too pale, too thin and far from clean, but Mrs. Rosevear loved boys and had a large charity for their almost perpetual grubbiness.

"What's your name?" she asked with a friendly smile. Surprised but flattered, Johnny smiled back and told her.

"Johnny—Johnny Connell."

"Well, Johnny, I'm just moving in. Like to come in and see what you think of the place?"

Johnny made no answer but stepped across the low brick wall that divided his front path from hers and she came and let him in. Johnny looked about him and gasped. Fresh primrose paint was on the walls, daffodil paint shone spotless on the woodwork while along the passage and up the stairs ran a strip of deep green carpet. Through the open door of the front room he saw the same paint and a primrose paper; a square of carpet was of a slightly lighter green patterned with fawn.

"Ain't that pretty?" marvelled Johnny, mentally comparing it with the dingy paint and worn oilcloth in his own home.

Mrs. Rosevear beamed. "Glad you like it," she said, then, waving towards the open door, "Come right in; maybe if you have nothing better to do you'll stay and talk for a bit?"

Johnny was glad of the invitation. He had only yesterday lost the leadership of his gang to a boy who had recently moved into the district, Alfie Carter, who was reputed to carry a spring knife and to have been in trouble with the police. His father he did not expect to see until after closing time.

There were two chairs in the room, one loaded with pictures and photographs, but Mrs. Rosevear settled him in the other and resumed her task of tacking down the carpet. She told him that her brother was a greengrocer and had brought part of her things over in his van; he would bring the rest after he closed his shop tonight.

"He's ever so kind," she told him, "but he has a wife and four children to look after so he won't be able to stay long—ow!" She dropped the hammer and sucked her thumb. Johnny got up at once.

"Dad says women should never be trusted with a hammer," he assured her. "You just give me that; I'll finish the job!"

She protested but yielded. "My husband always used to do these jobs for me," she admitted. "I'm not very handy with tools, but the work's there and must be done."

Johnny shot a glance at her, wondering whether her husband had run away as his mother had done. She saw but misinterpreted the look.

"He was killed in a motor accident three months ago—some men stole a car and the police chased them. Stanley tried to throw Minnie clear—that's my little girl—but the car went over her foot and she had to have it off. Her back was hurt, too, so she has to rest a lot, but the doctors say she will get better and then they have promised her an artificial foot so she'll be able to walk all right, but it all takes time and patience."

"That was tough luck," said Johnny sympathetically, driving in the last tack and scrambling to his feet. "Any more jobs? What about these pictures? Want me to knock in nails for them?"

"Oh, if you would!" she cried gratefully. "I'll show you where I want them to go, then I can go and get the tea ready. You'll stay for tea, won't you?"

Johnny flushed and tried not to show how hungry he was. Breakfast had been one slice of bread and he had expected nothing more until Dad came home. Mrs. Rosevear had already drawn her own conclusions from his thinness and the air of neglect which betrayed a house that was certainly not a home. She smiled and went off to the kitchen, whence came very soon the appetizing smell of toast.

Johnny chose suitable nails, drove them in with the skill picked up from his father, a carpenter, and began unpacking the pictures, which were carefully tied up in newspaper. He hung a round mirror on the wall facing the window, a silver birch wood carpeted with bluebells and a bowl of red and cream roses in the recesses on either side of the fireplace, a picture of mountains reflected in a lake on the third wall, then stopped to think. The wedding photo over the fireplace, Mrs. Rosevear had said. Johnny unpacked it and looked at it. Mrs. Rosevear, younger and somewhat slimmer, was looking up with an expression of happy trust into the eyes of a tall man who was bending down slightly with an air of protecting tenderness. Johnny, who had known so little affection in his short life, looked at the photograph with a wistful heart-hunger that he could not have put into words. He was reluctant to hang the picture and when he had done so kept returning to it as he folded the papers and tidily knotted up the string. Mrs. Rosevear, coming to see whether he was ready for tea, caught and read that wistful expression and returned quietly to the kitchen to wipe her eyes before calling him.

"Poor lad, poor lad!" she thought to herself. "Well, he shall have our friendship and I'll see whether we can't make him a little happier."

She went into the other room to pick up Minnie and settle her in a comfortable chair, then called cheerfully,

"Tea's ready, Johnny."

Johnny came at once, but halted at the door, suddenly shy at the sight of Minnie, for he had had little to do with girls. Minnie saw, approved and remarked with a smile,

"I'm glad you've found someone nice already, Mummie darling; I was afraid I was going to be lonely here."

Johnny flushed and looked at Mrs. Rosevear but she only smiled and drew out a chair for him. Johnny opened incredulous eyes; the table held half a sponge cake, a plate of scones, one dish of butter and one of jam and now Mrs. Rosevear was taking from the oven a heaped plate of generously buttered toast and three hot plates, on each of which she placed a round of toast, putting back the remainder to keep hot.

"Now, Minnie," she said, sitting down. Minnie closed her eyes, folded her hands together and said,

> "Thank You, Lord, for food to eat,
> Thank You, Lord, for friendship sweet.
> Give us what You see is best;
> Bless our home and be our Guest."

Johnny listened quietly but with wonder in his heart. However, the others at once began to eat and he hungrily picked up his toast, enjoying it to the full and gladly accepting a second and then a third round. Minnie before her accident had obviously been a bonny, sturdy child and though there was at present a look of fragility in her pretty face she ate with a fair appetite.

The teapot was a generous brown earthenware article that easily supplied Johnny with a third cup and when he found that not only was he expected to eat two slices of sponge cake, but his two scones were to be spread with butter *and* jam, he decided that he could not remember such a meal, not even when Mum had been at home to cook. They had just finished and washed up when there was a knock at the front door.

"That will be George with the rest of the furniture,"

exclaimed Mrs. Rosevear, hurrying to the door. A man's voice boomed,

"Settling down nicely, Sis? Now tell me where you want these things."

"Can I help?" inquired Johnny eagerly. Mr. Robson started, then laughed.

"Picked up one new friend already, Annie? There never was anyone like you for making friends!"

"Yes, and he's been helping me—finished tacking the front room carpet, hung the pictures and wiped up while I washed the tea-things!" She led the way into the front room and waved a hand towards the pictures and mirror. Mr. Robson examined the nails, nodded approvingly and turned to Johnny.

"Well, youngster, I *could* manage the furniture on my own, but if you are willing to help, I'll not deny that there will be less chance of scratched paint or torn wallpaper."

Johnny straightened up importantly and they began together to unload the van and carry in the furniture, Mrs. Rosevear showing where each piece was to go. At last all was in position and Johnny looked round with shining eyes. Little of it was new but it had been lovingly tended and polished and was arranged with some thought for beauty as well as use.

Johnny looked at Mrs. Rosevear, wondering whether he ought to go now, but she sank into a chair by the settee where Minnie lay watching all that went on. Johnny sat near by, glad of a rest, for he had worked hard. Mrs. Rosevear smiled at him.

"You *have* been a help, Johnny. There isn't much left to do now and I could never have been so quick on my own. I hope you'll come and see us again soon—when there isn't so much work around!"

"You bet!" Johnny replied eagerly. "Why, I liked the work—it was fun—and you've been ever so kind to me."

They talked quietly until Johnny, happening to glance out of the window, saw his father lurch past and decided that he had better go home. Minnie said:

"Good-bye, Johnny next door; come again soon!"

Johnny was scarcely home before a neighbour tapped at Mrs. Rosevear's door.

"You being a stranger to the neighbourhood," she began when it was opened, "I thought I'd warn you against that good-for-nothing little rascal Johnny Connell."

Mrs. Rosevear put out a hand. "Please," she said, "I'm sure you mean it kindly, but Johnny has been as good as gold all the time he has been here. Let's give him a chance, shall we?"

The neighbour tossed her head. "Oh, if you can't take good advice, good luck to you! Hope you don't live to regret it!" And with an indignant sniff she marched back to her own doorway, where she gave her next-door neighbour a somewhat embroidered account of the incident.

Johnny, putting himself to bed a little later, paused by the window as a clear, childish voice floated through to him.

"Now I lay me down to sleep
I pray Thee, Lord, my soul to keep.
If I should die before I wake
I pray Thee, Lord, my soul to take."

Johnny remembered that Minnie had recited a verse before tea; the words he had forgotten, but they were nice, and so was this. He tried to memorize it. Now Minnie was speaking again.

"Mummie, Johnny's a nice boy, isn't he?"

No one had taught Johnny that there was anything wrong in listening to talk not meant for his ears, so he craned farther out of the window for the reply.

"He was a good boy to us today, wasn't he, chick?"

"Mummie, do you think, sometimes, when you have to be out at work, Johnny would come in and read to me?"

Johnny drew in his head hastily, turning a little red. Never before had he been ashamed that he could not read—did not, indeed, even know the whole alphabet! How could he escape Minnie's contempt if he had to confess? Yet how could he possibly learn to read? He crawled into bed and lay awake for a while, but drifted off to sleep without finding an answer. When he awoke, however, he remembered his problem and all at once an idea came; he would ask one of the masters at school if there was any way to learn. Not Mr. Hardy, he decided at once—a sarcastic, quick-tempered man, making no secret of his contempt for Johnny. Not Mr. Jackson, who, the minute school was over, roared off on his motor-bike. His choice fell on Mr. Earnshaw, who took the carpentry class and thought rather well of Johnny's work.

So it came about that on Monday, instead of rushing out with the other boys during the break, Johnny went to the carpentry classroom and was glad to find Mr. Earnshaw alone.

"Please, sir," he ventured.

Mr. Earnshaw was checking some figures; he looked up rather absently, murmured, "Yes, Johnny?" and looked back at his papers. Johnny tried again.

"Please, sir, do you think——"

Mr. Earnshaw was a kindly man; he pushed aside his papers and turned to Johnny, saying, "Yes, my boy; do I think—what?"

The words came with a rush now. "Do you think I could learn to read?"

Mr. Earnshaw looked at Johnny, took off his spectacles to look again and suggested quietly, "Suppose you tell me, Johnny?"

Johnny didn't find it very easy to tell but somehow, in a jumbled way, he made Mr Earnshaw understand that there were new neighbours next door who had been kind to him, that the little girl had lost her Dad and her foot in a car accident and that she wanted Johnny to read to her. Mr. Earnshaw had been thinking fast while Johnny spoke; now, carefully looking out of the window, he asked,

"Is there any reason why you should go straight home tonight?"

Johnny's voice was expressionless as he replied,

"No, sir; there's nobody there when I get in."

"Do you know Silverdale Road? You do? Good. Don't be too quick to leave school tonight, walk slowly towards Silverdale Road and I'll catch you up about the time you get there. We don't want everyone to know that we have a secret, do we?"

Johnny thanked him and hurried away. Mr. Earnshaw sat with a rather grim expression, adding to what Johnny had said much that he had left unsaid, piecing it out with what he knew of the boy in school and concluding that there might be more in him than anyone had imagined—for, after all, when there are thirty to fifty boys in a class, it is difficult to give any of them individual attention.

Chapter 2

A NEW AMBITION

JOHNNY did not find it easy to obey Mr. Earnshaw's instructions about going slowly, but worked off his impatience by practising a rather complicated tap-dance as he went along. On reaching the corner of Silverdale Road he glanced back and saw that Mr. Earnshaw had just turned the last corner and was coming towards him with a friendly smile. Together they turned in at No. 27, entering a big, rather austere front room where Mr. Earnshaw took from a drawer a pack of cards and handed them to Johnny, drawing out a chair by the table and saying,

"Now I want you to sort out all the letters you are quite sure you know."

Johnny found that each card had a large capital letter on its front and, sitting down to the task, he began sorting them into little heaps, while his teacher went to the kitchen and prepared two large cups of cocoa and some cheese sandwiches. With these he returned to the front room as Johnny finished. There was one unhesitating line, A, B, C, D, E, F, G followed by several not in rows. Mr. Earnshaw leaned over and read, T, R, K, I, L, X, M, O, S, U. Setting cocoa and sandwiches before Johnny, he sipped his own cup, puzzling over the letters.

"Can you tell me," he asked at last, "why those particular letters?"

Johnny considered. "Well, sir, we always begin at A, don't we? I kind of lose interest after I get to G."

"And the others? This, for instance?" He touched the X.

"They put that in the picture papers to mark the spot where things happen."

"Oh, of course," said Mr. Earnshaw. "And the rest?"

For answer, Johnny began lifting cards from the piles and spelling words—rice, sugar, flour, tea, milk. "Mum used to tell me to get them for her," he explained, "and she hit me if I made mistakes."

"You say your mother *used* to tell you—is she dead?"

Johnny's face went blank. "No, sir."

Mr. Earnshaw set down his cup, went to the bookcase that took up most of one wall and chose a beautifully illustrated copy of *Andersen's Fairy Tales*.

"Look at this book," he said, laying it before Johnny, who turned over the leaves, exclaiming over each picture.

"It is June now; if you can learn to read this by December, you shall have it and I will leave you quite free either to keep it yourself or, if you wish, give it to your new friend as a Christmas present."

"You don't mean it, sir?" Johnny looked up, hardly daring to believe, but as he read the answer in Mr. Earnshaw's face, his whole expression changed to steady determination. Mr. Earnshaw set aside the letters that Johnny already knew, picked up and named again and again those of which he was unsure, then began jumping from known to unknown letters and back. Treated as a game, it seemed easier than it had ever done in school and before long he was confidently naming every one.

Next Mr. Earnshaw opened his piano, played a simple tune and began to sing the alphabet. Johnny had a quick ear for a tune and soon picked it up; getting the letters right was not quite so easy until Mr. Earnshaw allied eye to ear, setting the alphabet in order, line by line, on the table and playing the tune slower so that Johnny could follow the letters.

"Now," he said at last, satisfied, "you run along home singing it to yourself—oh, and Johnny, there are plenty of advertisements whose pictures give you a clue to what they are; see how many of them you can read. When would you like to come here again?"

"Tomorrow?" pleaded Johnny, greatly daring. Mr. Earnshaw laughed and agreed and Johnny ran off home, stopping beside every advertisement he passed to study the letters and try to understand them.

Mr. Earnshaw could not spare time for him every evening but invited him often enough for real progress; in between, Johnny made his way to Mrs. Rosevear and Minnie. Between them, he was learning more than the alphabet. He was observant enough when anything interested him and he began to pay more attention to cleanliness and tried to show his gratitude for the friendship shown him by little services. He helped Mrs. Rosevear to dig up the neglected little garden, learned to plant out the seedlings she brought home and to water, weed and rake. When flowers began to appear, he hung over each with as much excitement as his neighbours. Finding something to do for Mr. Earnshaw was not so easy but, as he grew more familiar with the household, he noticed that the daily cleaner did not consider shoes to be her responsibility—and that Mr. Earnshaw hated shoe-cleaning! From that moment, Johnny took over the task and produced such a shine that someone asked Mr. Earnshaw whether he was courting!

The lessons continued during part of the school holidays; even when Mr. Earnshaw was away in the Lake District, Johnny went on using the posters as lesson-books. He was becoming reasonably sure of winning the book by Christmas and was even looking forward with some interest to the new term at school, for Mr. Earnshaw picked out for his reading lessons short, easy passages from beautifully illustrated books and would then let him look at the pictures, arousing his interest in geography by glimpses of other lands and nations, in botany by plates of wild flowers, some of which he recognized as growing on local bomb sites, in natural history by books on animals, birds, insects, and, one wonderful Saturday, by a visit to the Zoo. The friendship did much for Johnny; it was also of value to Mr. Earnshaw, a widower whose only son had been killed in the war. He had tended to shut himself in with his beloved books and lose touch with people, but the realization of Johnny's need had opened his eyes to his own growing selfishness and he had diffidently offered his help to the minister of his church, and had been astounded by the eagerness with which that overworked man accepted it.

The holidays had brought much extra work to Mrs. Rosevear who, having become known as a thoroughly reliable domestic worker, was being asked not only to look after flats while their owners were away, but to do temporary work while other daily helps took their holidays. She planned to take Minnie to a cousin in Brighton for a fortnight in September; meanwhile she was worrying because she could not take the child out so often in her wheeled chair. She consulted Johnny, who fought against panic as he thought of the jeers of his former gang. It took real courage to offer to wheel the chair himself, but he could not forget how much happiness they had brought him and felt that it was only fair to help where he could.

The next day it rained heavily, but the day after was warm and sunny. Johnny carefully helped Minnie into her chair, tucked her rug round her and set out. They had not gone far before one of his old friends saw him and swooped to the attack.

"Yah! Look at Johnny Nursie!" he yelled. Another boy heard him and joined in and between them they managed to call up most of the local boys, including

Alfie. He, too, took up the cry, and Minnie began to be frightened. Johnny had an inspiration.

"Don't see none of *you* being trusted with her," he declared loftily. Alfie gaped and looked at Minnie.

"What's so special about her?" he inquired.

"What'll you give me to tell you?" countered Johnny.

Alfie went through his pockets, surveying and thrusting back the usual boy assortment until he reached a paper bag.

"Gob-stopper?" he suggested, offering one.

"Not that one," said Johnny briefly. "You been sucking it."

Alfie stared. "Choosy, ain't yer?" he commented. He still had the bag in his hand and with one lightning, continuous movement Johnny snatched it, selected a sweet, popped it in Minnie's astonished mouth and returned the bag just as Alfie moved forward to exact vengeance. Finding the sweets in his own hand again, he stared stupidly. Brawn rather than brain had brought him to gang leadership and he was baffled by Johnny's quick thinking. He turned to look at Minnie, sucking happily, and remembered that the sweet was to have been payment for value received.

"Well," he said truculently, "*what* is it that's so special?"

Minnie bent forward and drew aside the rug, exposing the pathetic little bandaged stump. Alfie's lawlessness was due far more to lack of imagination than to actual cruelty; the sight of the mutilated leg woke a spark of pity in him. Suspecting that this might be taken for weakness, he suddenly rounded on his gang, snarling,

"Let me find *one* of you lay a finger on Johnny or the kid and I'll bash his face in! See?"

They saw. Actually, they saw more than he meant them to see, for more than one was finding a curious difficulty in swallowing, and even one of the less sensitive murmured that it was "tough on the little 'un" and wanted to know how it happened. Minnie explained, simply and sweetly, and when it came home to them that her father had risked and lost his life to save her, a little of the glamour faded from their favourite film stars and clung instead to Mr. Rosevear. Johnny did not yet know it, but Minnie had gained a little band of protectors who were to make life easier for her in more ways than one.

School term began and on the first Friday Johnny hurried home because on the following day the Rosevears were off to Brighton. Mrs. Rosevear, knowing that Johnny was due home soon, had tucked Minnie into her chair and left her in the tiny front garden while she went to one last job. Here an idle bully discovered her and, the street being empty at the moment, amused himself by pinching her and pulling her hair. She began to cry and Johnny, rounding the last corner, heard her and darted forward with an indignant shout. The bully looked round but, being twice Johnny's size, went on teasing. Alfie, however, had heard Johnny and, his curiosity roused, followed in time to see him fling himself on the stranger. Guessing what was wrong, he gave the piercing whistle that was the rallying call of the gang. One appeared, then two or three more. Led by Alfie, they attacked just as the bully sent Johnny spinning with a blow on the jaw. He was surrounded before he knew it; punches and kicks landed in front, behind and on both sides and when he tried to hit back his blows usually landed where a boy had been a second or two earlier. Breaking through them, he ran, pursued with exultant yelps by all but Johnny, who was more concerned about Minnie. The gang harried their victim until Alfie spotted a policeman in the distance and whistled them back. With a jerk of his thumb he gave the order to disappear, and by the time the patrolling policeman reached the corner the only boy in sight was Johnny, comforting a child who was already beginning to smile.

"Thank you, Johnny, for being so brave," she said, "but oh, I *am* glad those other boys helped. Did he hurt you much?"

Johnny made light of his bruises and presently Minnie suggested that he should go and thank the others.

"Yes, if you like," he replied, and waited only until he saw Mrs. Rosevear coming, then set off for Alfie's house.

Alfie's father answered his knock, and when Johnny asked to see the lad, he shouted over his shoulder,

"Alfie, here's someone asking for you; what you bin up to now?"

Alfie, all injured innocence, came forward, protesting, "I ain't done nothing!" but on catching sight of Johnny he turned dusky red and backed away. His father grabbed him by the collar.

"So you ain't done nothing! You look like it, I must say!"

Johnny tugged at Mr. Carter's arm. "It wasn't the way you think. A man was hurting a little girl I know so I tried to stop him and Alfie helped and she said to thank him!"

He kept his hold on the collar, looking from one to the other.

"You pulling a fast one?" he queried suspiciously.

"Honest, Mr. Carter! You can ask Minnie, if you like!"

Alfie hung his head, far more ashamed of detection in his one good deed than of all the mischief that had gone before. His father loosened his grip on the collar and held out his hand.

"Alfie, my boy, shake! I didn't think you had it in you!"

Alfie reluctantly shook hands and fled. Johnny, feeling that he had done what was required of him, went back to Minnie and tried not to spoil her pleasure in the coming holiday by any hint of his own loneliness. He did, however, find out their Brighton address and say airily that he might send them a postcard if he was not too busy!

Chapter 3

BY THE SEA

MRS. ROSEVEAR had considered the extravagance of a taxi to Victoria, but Johnny was really shocked by this, pointing out that they could get a bus all the way from the corner and that he could easily wheel Minnie to the 'bus stop in her chair and bring it back to the house afterwards. After some discussion this was agreed as, although Mrs. Rosevear had received a fair sum in compensation for her husband's death and spent generously on all that she considered necessary, she had no intention of wasting any of it.

The luggage consisted of one large suitcase, which was tied to the chair, and a smaller one, which Mrs. Rosevear carried. They set out in ample time and Johnny untied the case and watched for a not too full 'bus with a kind-looking conductor. He was, for his age, a shrewd judge of character, and when he was satisfied and asked for the needed help the man picked up Minnie and seated her safely while Johnny put the big case under the stairs. Mrs. Rosevear climbed in with the other case, thanking Johnny and waving until they were out of sight; he then carefully wheeled the chair back and put it in the house. Next, proud of the key with which he had been trusted, he tied it on string and hung it round his neck for safety. He had promised to water the flowers when necessary, so he wandered into the garden and removed a weed or two, but there had been rain in the night and he found little to do. It was a lonely week-end. On Monday after school he went to Mr. Earnshaw for another lesson, but was so obviously low-spirited that his teacher asked the reason and, on hearing it, looked at him thoughtfully for a while.

"See here, Johnny," he suggested at last, "if you will write a postcard to say we are coming and ask if we may meet them, I'll take you to Brighton for the day next Saturday!"

Johnny gazed at him absolutely speechless, and Mr. Earnshaw laughed and fetched a postcard and a stamp. He advised Johnny to write out first what he wanted to say then copy it on to the card. Johnny agreed eagerly, for even now it seemed a formidable task to compose a letter, however brief. He needed a little help, but at last produced his completed card.

Dear Mrs. Rosevear,

Mr. Earnshaw says if it would not bother you to see me he could bring me down to Brighton on Saturday. I miss you both and I have never seen the sea but I do not want to bother you. It is very kind of Mr. Earnshaw.

Yours truly,

Johnny next door.

Mr. Earnshaw smiled a little, but affixed the stamp and sent Johnny out to the post-box at once, when they settled down happily to their lesson. The reply came when Mr. Connell was out, so no explanations were needed.

Dear Johnny,

It will be lovely to see you. You had better come to us here as we are quite close to the station and we do not know what the weather will be like.

Love from us both,
Annie and Minnie Rosevear.

It was a coloured picture-card and Johnny studied it till he knew every detail, trying to imagine what it would be like to be there. Saturday proved one of those softly glorious days that can come in mid-September. Mr. Earnshaw had tactfully found out what time Mr. Connell left home in the morning and arranged to meet Johnny a quarter of an hour later. Determined to make the most of the occasion, he had obtained the tickets beforehand and risen early to pack a basket of food—sandwiches, buns, hard-boiled eggs, chocolate and fruit. He had booked corner seats, looking forward with some interest to watching Johnny's face, as he knew that the boy had never been farther than Hampstead Heath.

As soon as they reached the country, Johnny observed and commented freely.

"There's an awful lot of empty places," he remarked disapprovingly. "It's kind of pretty, but you'd think they'd use some of them instead of jamming all the houses up together like they are our way!"

"People do live here, Johnny," explained Mr. Earnshaw; "farmers who need fields to grow your food. Look, that's a field of cabbages. Those trees bear the apples you see in the shops. Sheep need fields to make the wool for your clothes and the mutton you eat—cows need good pasture to make milk, butter, cheese, beef, leather for your shoes."

Johnny was intensely interested. "Do show me a cow," he begged. "I've seen sheep in the Park but I've never seen a cow!" However, on seeing one, he declared that he preferred his milk out of a bottle!

Presently Mr. Earnshaw unpacked his basket and offered refreshments. When they had eaten, Johnny sat looking at Mr. Earnshaw with a sober, intent expression and soon his teacher asked what was on his mind.

"I was wondering," he ventured, "why you are so kind to me?"

Mr. Earnshaw smiled. "There are several reasons, I think. I don't believe you have had a square deal and I like to see people treated fairly. Then I find I like you; it gives me pleasure to see you enjoying yourself. You appreciate what is done for you and you show it. I doubt whether many boys would have troubled to notice that I don't like shoe-cleaning!"

Johnny grinned bashfully. "Any more reasons?"

"Yes, Johnny. I haven't spoken about it much because here *I* am a learner. I am a Christian and as such I ought to love and serve others, but when I lost my wife and my only son, I selfishly shut myself away from people and you have shown me that I was wrong."

Johnny looked thoughtful. "Like when Minnie says 'Now I lay me down to sleep'?" he inquired. He had heard this many times and now knew it by heart.

"Yes, Johnny, just like that."

Johnny became silent, thinking things over, and in a few more minutes they were at Brighton. They were directed to a pleasant street of small houses and presently Johnny broke into a run as he saw Minnie leaning out of an open window. She fairly shrieked with excitement when she saw him.

"Johnny, what *do* you think? You'll never guess! I can swim!"

"Go on!" said Johnny, half unbelieving, but she turned to her mother, who had now come to the window, and Mrs. Rosevear nodded triumphantly.

"Not very far, of course, but even a little is doing her such a lot of good. Is that your friend Mr. Earnshaw, Johnny? I'll open the door and then you can hear all about it."

They were introduced to Mrs. Killearn and the children—Peter, who was just thirteen, Paul, about Johnny's age, and the twins, Sylvia and Sarella, who were a little younger than Minnie. Mr. Earnshaw suggested leaving Johnny with them and calling for him in time for the train back, but Mrs. Killearn objected at once. "Not unless you've business down here and *must* leave us. We've heard about you and my husband will be disappointed if he doesn't meet you and I'm sure Minnie will be upset if you don't meet the doctor—eh, my pet?"

"You don't even know about the doctor yet," exclaimed Minnie, "and he taught me to swim!"

Mr. Earnshaw sat down beside her. "You must tell me about this; it sounds almost too good to be true."

"It all began our very first day down here. Uncle Harry carried me down to the beach and the others brought rugs and sandwiches and tea, then Uncle had to go to his boat—he takes people out in it—and we sat and talked and looked at the sea and presently ever such a nice man came and asked the twins and me if we would like to play with his little girls. I told him I couldn't play because of my foot and he was so kind and called Rosemary and Marigold and they knew lots of sitting-down games and we had such fun! Then he said he was a doctor and asked if he might see how bad my foot was and when he had looked he said that he was taking his little girls for a swim and if I would come, too, he would take care of me and teach me to swim."

"At first I was a bit troubled," put in Mrs. Rosevear, "but he said it would do her good and he would not let her stay in long enough to be a strain, and Marigold even had a spare bathing costume that fitted well enough with a safety-pin at the waist, but she got on so well that on the way home I bought her one of her own."

Minnie took up the story again. "It's scarlet with white seagulls on it! First, Marigold showed me what to do with my arms and legs, then we changed into our swim-suits and the doctor held me up while I practised—and I love it! I didn't want to come out, but the doctor said I must be careful at first, and now he doesn't have to hold me up any more because I can swim all by myself."

A car hooted outside. "That will be the doctor now," declared Mrs. Rosevear. "We told him you were coming and we might be late on the beach and he said Minnie ought to bathe while the tide was right and if we were not down in good time he would come up here."

The doctor sent Marigold to ask whether they were ready, and after a short discussion it was decided that Minnie and Johnny should go in the car and the others follow. Johnny was hastily provided with a bathing slip and a towel, Minnie proudly showed her scarlet costume, then they were off. It was only a short run; almost at once Johnny was gazing astounded at a great dazzle of water shining in the sun and gasping, "Is that the sea? Coo, ain't there a lot of it?"

The doctor laughed, drew in to the kerb, put Minnie on a seat and told them not to go down on the beach until he had parked the car. By the time he was back, the rest of the party had caught up and the doctor carried Minnie down to the beach. Very soon all were in the water except Mrs. Rosevear, who preferred to be ready to help Minnie when she came out. Johnny, who had learnt to swim with his school-mates in the local baths, was a little nervous of the waves but, seeing Minnie go in so confidently, he would not confess it but waded out, shivering a little, then struck out as he had been taught and was pleasantly surprised to find himself swimming better than in the baths. The twins, plump and placid, stayed on the edge, the doctor kept close to Minnie, while Peter, who was a strong swimmer, challenged Mr. Earnshaw to a race. Paul, a mischievous bit of quicksilver, dashed all over the place, now in the water, now out.

Presently Mrs. Rosevear took a towel and threw it round Paul, saying with a chuckle.

"I think ices all round would be a good idea!"

"Definitely," agreed the doctor, who liked ice-cream as well as anyone, so Mrs. Rosevear gave Paul the money and he ran off to their favourite shop while the others dried and dressed themselves. Johnny ate his ice and, licking the last creamy traces from his fingers, murmured,

"Boy, oh boy! *What* a day!"

"Anything special about it?" asked the doctor.

"Special!" exploded Johnny, "Well, I'll say! First time I've been outside London, or on a train—except the Underground—or in a car, or seen the sea and swum in it, or met so many nice people—and Mr. Earnshaw bringing food to eat on the train—oh, and first time I've seen a cow—though I didn't think much of it—sheep are prettier!" He stopped breathless and the doctor laughed.

The whole day was wonderful, but for Johnny the best part of all came after tea when Mr. Killearn came home. He had been a sailor during the war and had a jolly sunburnt face and an apparently endless fund of stories, but what captivated Johnny was that as soon as he came in he picked up a piece of wood and a knife and began carving a little ship. Johnny watched enthralled as it began to take shape but when Mr. Killearn, noticing his interest, laid aside his work and gave Johnny a completed model with masts and sails, he could hardly find words to voice his thanks. Mr. Earnshaw, watching, wondered whether there were any wood-carving classes where Johnny could learn; since his carpentry was well above average and he was obviously sensitive to beauty, perhaps wood-carving would prove his real bent.

When they had said good-bye and were on the train home, Johnny tried to talk about his day, but so much had been crowded into so short a time that he was really tired out and slept most of the way home, only rousing as they neared Victoria to lift down his precious ship from the luggage rack and thank Mr. Earnshaw for the most wonderful day of his life.

Chapter 4

STREET ACCIDENT

EVEN so casual a parent as Mr. Connell could not help noticing that Johnny was changing. He watched suspiciously for a while and, having seen his son working in the garden next door, he stopped Mrs. Rosevear and asked,

"Is that young rascal of mine giving you any trouble?"

"Trouble?" echoed Mrs. Rosevear, astonished. "Whatever gave you that idea? Johnny is a real good friend and a great help; we are glad to have him whenever he likes to come."

Mr. Connell gave her a bewildered look and went indoors to think things over. He remembered that none of the neighbours had recently stopped him, as they had so often done in the past, to complain of Johnny's misdeeds. Now he began to take notice of him and realized that the lad was growing fast; his only suit was not only shabby but quite obviously getting too small for him. Rather to his own surprise, he decided that Johnny not only needed a new suit—he deserved it. With a strength of mind of which he had not thought himself capable, on the next few pay-days he went straight to a friend of his in the tailoring line and handed over part of his pay-packet. When he had reached the sum they had agreed between themselves, he took Johnny round to the shop and chose a strong, serviceable suit in charcoal grey.

He looked Johnny over, but sighed heavily. The new suit showed up painfully how shabby was everything else. The socks and shirt, thanks to Mrs. Rosevear's busy needle, did not look too bad, but the suit was so obviously the only new thing that Mr. Connell turned appealingly to his friend.

"Bill," he begged, "will you finish the job and trust me for the rest of the money?"

Bill hesitated, but trade was not too good and he would not miss a sale. He told them plainly that he would charge extra for a credit sale, but he honestly searched through his stocks for hard-wearing things of the right size and Johnny walked proudly out of the shop, new-clothed from head to foot. As soon as he could, he slipped in next door to show himself and when they had exclaimed and admired, he said eagerly,

"Sometimes Dad goes out of a Sunday. Next time he does—now I look a bit respectable—could I—could I come to church with you?"

"Why, of course, Johnny!" Mrs. Rosevear was no believer in forcing religion on any child, but she did most steadfastly believe that if she lived her faith to the utmost of her power and prayed for those she loved, they must sooner or later come of their own free will. She had been praying for Johnny ever since their first meeting.

However, before that first visit to church, something

else happened that brought about many changes. It was on a sunny, mild Saturday afternoon in late October that Johnny took Minnie out in her wheel-chair. They were bound for a little park with a pond where Johnny, who had been whittling away for weeks at a rough copy of his precious model boat, wanted to see whether it would sail. Minnie was carrying the boat while Johnny gave his attention chiefly to the chair, and they were chattering away so eagerly that Johnny did not notice his mother on the opposite side of the road, coming towards them, none too steadily, arm in arm with a man. Mrs. Connell, however, saw her son and exclaimed,

"Why, there's my Johnny! Hey, Johnny!"

He did not hear her, and suddenly she pulled herself free of her companion and darted across the road. Johnny heard the grinding screech of brakes too hastily applied and looked up to see his mother in the path of a car. With a wild cry of "Mum!" he darted towards her, but a man with rough kindness seized his arm and swung him round so that he did not see the actual impact. He struggled to free himself, but the man told him,

"No use, sonny; you couldn't have done a thing and we should have had two of you under the car instead of one."

Johnny looked up. "Oh, it's you, Mr. Carter. Would you look after Minnie for me"—he pointed to the chair—"because I must go to Mum?"

A white-faced driver climbed out of the car. "I

couldn't help it," he appealed, teeth chattering with shock, to the crowd already gathering. "You all saw I couldn't avoid her—she ran right in front of me."

"That's right, mate," said a man wearing a Red Cross badge. "We'll need tackle to get the car off her; you can't go back or forward without doing more harm. Someone dial 999 and ask for police, ambulance and fire-brigade with lifting tackle."

Someone ran to the telephone at the corner. Johnny had fought his way through the crowd and knelt beside his mother, crying desperately,

"Mum! Mum! Are you hurt bad? Speak to me!"

Mrs. Connell opened her eyes. "'Lo, Johnny," she whispered, then, wonderingly, "Why, Johnny, you're crying!"

Johnny hastily wiped his eyes with the back of his hand and turned to the man kneeling beside him. "Is she hurt bad, mister? It's my Mum."

The man looked sympathetically at him, nodded slightly and began giving instructions to those around him.

"Something warm to cover her, please."

The driver opened the car door and offered a cushion and a travelling rug. The man, using them skilfully, asked,

"Can someone provide hot, very sweet tea, please?"

"I can," said a woman. "I'd only just poured the water on the leaves when I heard the brakes and saw the car hit her." She and a neighbour hurried off and came back with a tray which they brought to the man who had taken charge. He noted that there were two cups, lavishly sugared both, and offering one to the still shaking driver he held the other to Mrs. Connell's lips. She took a sip or two but soon turned her head aside to look again at Johnny.

"Why should you care?" she asked. "I've been a bad mother to you—and a bad wife to your Dad."

"You're *my* Mum," said Johnny.

The first-aider's hands were gently exploring and testing, but spasms of pain and smothered groans told him that the damage was beyond his power to help. Mrs. Connell, drawing short, painful breaths, was beginning to look frightened. She turned to Johnny again. "Johnny, I've been a bad woman, but if *you* can forgive me, maybe God would, if I could only think of a prayer to ask Him. I never taught you to pray, did I?"

"I know the one Minnie says every night," he told her; "'Now I lay me down to sleep——'"

"'Now—I lay me—down—to sleep.' I used to say that when I was your age, Johnny. How does it go on?"

"I pray Thee, Lord, my soul to keep."

"I—pray Thee, Lord—my soul—to keep," she whispered.

"If I should die before I wake——"

A sudden radiant smile lit her face. Unprompted, she gasped,

"I pray Thee, Lord—my soul—to take."

With a little sigh she relaxed into the lovely tranquillity of death. The man beside her covered the still face and rose to his feet. In the silence they heard the distant sound of a fire-engine bell, followed almost at once by the softer tinkle of the ambulance. Just before they arrived, a policeman took charge and with calm authority moved on all except actual witnesses. While he took particulars, the firemen lifted the car and the ambulance men, bringing a stretcher, carried her to the ambulance. The Red Cross man, having given his name and address, gently drew Johnny away and offered to see him home, but, finding that Minnie was still near by, the lad roused himself to look after her and was relieved to find that, although she knew of his mother's death, she had been allowed to see nothing. Mr. Carter had been standing between her and the car when the accident happened and as the crowd gathered he had wheeled her away.

One of the bystanders knew where Mr. Connell worked and hurried round to report the death to the manager, who, after consultation with the owners of the firm, sent for him.

"What have I done now?" he protested, but the messenger knew nothing and Mr. Connell stumped along to the manager's room, wondering uneasily whether he was to be sacked. Instead, he was told of his wife's death, granted leave of absence until after the funeral, and sent in one of the firm's cars to the hospital where Mrs. Connell's body had been taken. In death, she looked so like the girl he had courted and married that he broke down and wept. As he made his way home, one neighbour after another stopped him to offer sympathy and help, and, as they spoke of the accident, he was astounded to hear from several the story of Johnny's prayer.

"Good as a parson, he was," said one who had stood very near, "and you know what? She smiled—really smiled, as though she'd seen someone she was ever so glad to see, and went off to sleep as peaceful as a child holding her Mammy's hand—only it wasn't sleep, it was death."

Mr. Connell, not finding Johnny at home, guessed that he might be with the Rosevears, and paused only long enough to draw down his blinds before tapping on their door. Mrs. Rosevear welcomed him in and took him to Johnny, who was lying down, muffled in blankets, but shivering.

"It's shock," explained the little widow. "He thought first of Minnie and brought her safely home, then I persuaded him to lie down and I've put both kettles on for a hot bottle and a pot of tea. Would you care for a cup?"

"Thank you, ma'am, I would indeed. It's been a shock to me, too, I can tell you, and all the worse that I keep on thinking that if I'd taken better care of her she'd be alive now."

"That's not for me to pry into," replied Mrs. Rosevear gently, "but if you feel that way, make it up by looking after Johnny better, will you?"

"If Johnny'll let me," he assured her with a new

humility. She left him for a few minutes, came back with a hot bottle for Johnny, went off again to make the tea and was soon back with a tray, pouring cups for them all. Johnny stopped shivering and reached out to clasp his father's hand.

Chapter 5

JOHNNY AND HIS DAD

WHEN Johnny woke next morning, his father was sitting by his bed. Johnny sat up, startled.

"Hello, Dad! What's up?" Then he remembered and lay down again, hiding his face in his pillow. Yesterday he had actually cried in public; today he must show more control.

"Johnny," said his father heavily, "I bin a fool; I bin a fool, Johnny. If I'd a took proper care of her, your Mum might be alive now. A woman needs a man to look after her, especially a pretty one, and your Mum was a smashing pretty girl."

"Yes, Dad," agreed Johnny, puzzled but interested.

"All this drinking, too," continued Mr. Connell. "You spend all your money and what do you get? A head like a hammer knocking on your skull and a mouth like the bottom of a bird-cage! And now I've got nothing put by to bury her decent. Johnny, my lad, I'm going to give up the drink, you see if I don't. But you'll have to help me, Johnny. Drink gets a hold of you, like. It isn't going to be easy."

Johnny looked somewhat doubtful; other heavy drinkers in the locality had sworn off drink in the morning and been back in the pub by evening. Mr. Connell saw the look.

"They was telling me," he observed humbly, "that when your Mum died you told her a prayer to say that helped her. *I* never taught you no prayers and I'm dead certain *she* never did. Who taught you to pray, Johnny? Couldn't they help me?"

"It was Minnie's prayer," said Johnny slowly. "She didn't exactly teach it to me; I just heard her say it and liked it, so I learnt it. I guess her Mum taught her."

"Mrs. Rosevear," mused Mr. Connell. "Well, she certainly spoke to me straight about looking after you. Real kind she was, though. I don't believe I'd be scared to speak to her. Is it her what's made *you* so different?"

Johnny considered. "I suppose so—partly her and partly Mr. Earnshaw. They've both been ever so kind."

Mr. Connell, who knew nothing about Mr. Earnshaw, asked a good many questions, exclaiming at last,

"Well, it begins to seem as if I don't know much about my own son. I reckon your pals next door don't think much of me. I—I don't think I'd better speak to them, after all!"

There was a knock at the front door; Mr. Connell, going to answer it, found Mrs. Rosevear holding a covered dish.

"I've cooked you a bit of breakfast as I heard voices. It ought to be eaten at once, or it'll spoil."

Mr. Connell looked at her open-mouthed, but she

walked serenely past him, set her dish on a chest of drawers beside Johnny and, removing two hot plates, set on each a liberal helping of fried egg, bacon and fried bread and was off with the empty dish before either of them could do more than stammer a word or two of thanks. They were no more than half-way through the meal before she was back with two steaming cups of coffee. This time, as she was about to go, Mr. Connell summoned up courage to ask her to stay a minute. "There's something I want to ask you, ma'am," he said. She hesitated.

"Finish your breakfast first, then; I'm just looking after Minnie. You can say whatever you want to say when I collect the washing-up."

They ate in silence, Johnny because he was hungry, Mr. Connell because he was thinking uneasily of what he wanted to say and how to open the subject. Johnny went into the kitchen to wash, dress and run a comb through his hair and opened the door to Mrs. Rosevear as she came back.

"Now," she said briskly, gathering her things, "what is it you want to ask? I'll do what I can."

"Thank you," replied Mr. Connell; "it's just that—well—I——"

He stumbled into silence and Johnny came to his rescue. "Dad wants to give up the drink and he thought maybe——"

Mr. Connell looked at her wistfully. "It isn't going to be easy, I know that. I thought maybe—a—a prayer would help?"

Mrs. Rosevear impulsively patted his shoulder. "I'm real glad to hear you say that," she told him, "and I don't know anything better than prayer for seeing you through trouble. I've seen enough of what the drink can do never to touch it myself, and my husband was the same. I'll pray for you gladly and my Minnie will, too, I know." And picking up her things, she whisked off home. Mr. Connell looked after her, a little disappointed.

"I thought she would have taught me a bit of something to say myself. *You* don't know one for me, do you, Johnny?"

"Only Minnie's prayer," replied Johnny, repeating it, but Mr. Connell would have none of it.

"No, no, my boy; there's nothing about drink in that, and as for that bit about dying, we've had one death in the family and we don't want no more. Anyhow, I ain't fit to die yet."

In such neighbourhoods as that where Johnny lived, there is much kindness in times of sorrow. A workmate came round with money collected in the firm, someone in the street gathered in a pound or two, and Mr. Connell had the sense to hand it over at once to the undertaker in part payment of the funeral expenses. The drama of her death resulted in a really astonishing display of flowers, and many were present at the service, which took place at Mrs. Rosevear's church, as Mrs. Connell had not been inside a church since Johnny was christened. Mr. Connell could not remember his last church attendance; he had been in the army and unable to get leave for the christening and had been married at the registrar's office. The minister made the fullest possible use of the opportunity, and at least some of the seed sown sprang up.

On their return home after the funeral, Johnny looked at his father.

"Dad," he said, "you remember what you said about not being fit to die? Dad, was Mum fit to die?"

Mr. Connell scratched his head uneasily. "Well, I don't rightly know, Johnny," he admitted. "I don't understand these things. She done plenty she didn't ought to, but Mrs. Glover down the road told me that after she said your prayer she smiled like she was smiling at a friend and died peaceful and happy. I reckon you'd better ask your pals next door."

Johnny took his advice at once but to his astonishment found Mrs. Rosevear in tears.

"I'll come some other time," he muttered uneasily, but she replied,

"No, come in, Johnny; it's stupid of me, but I was just thinking, supposing it had been me instead of your mother, what would become of Minnie?"

Johnny thought it over, then gave his opinion. "Dad says every woman needs a man to look after her, so if anything happened to you, I guess I'd better marry Minnie and take care of her!"

"Why, Johnny!" gasped Mrs. Rosevear, and again "Why, Johnny!" Her tears were forgotten and she turned hastily away to hide the laughter in her eyes.

"It's real sweet of you, Johnny," she managed at last; "let's hope nothing happens to me just yet—you're a bit young for the responsibilities of marriage!"

Johnny squared his shoulders. "I'm not afraid of responsibility," he boasted airily, adding more thoughtfully, "'Sides, it isn't as if we'd be on our own, is it? Minnie's God would look after us, wouldn't He?"

Both laughter and tears were utterly forgotten now. Mrs. Rosevear's eyes searched his earnest little face. Sitting down, she drew him to her.

"Johnny," she said softly, "you said 'Minnie's God'. Why not *your* God?"

Johnny flushed and looked down. "He wouldn't want me; I'm not good like you and Minnie."

"He came 'not to call the righteous, but sinners to repentance'," she quoted softly, but Johnny looked at her, bewildered.

"Who came?" he asked, "and what does that mean?"

"Jesus came, Johnny," she told him. "Don't you know about Jesus and about God?"

"Not much, except Christmas carols and what I've heard from you and Minnie. I always used to think it was sort of fairy stories, but you talk about God as if He was real."

"I know He is real, Johnny dear. Nearly twelve years ago I lost my darling mother, and while I was nursing her I hadn't a doubt in my mind that she was going to Heaven, and I kept thinking of all the times I had disobeyed her or lost my temper with her and all the times when I wasn't as kind as I might have been—but she never lost her temper, just gave me a grieved look and presently she'd go into her own room and shut the door and I'd know she was praying for me. Poor mother, she never saw the answer to her prayers. It wasn't until I lost her, and the boy I was running around with threw me over and married his manager's daughter, and my health broke down, and I lost my job, that I stopped fighting for my own way and longed for the peace and joy I had seen in my mother's face."

"Yes, that's it," exclaimed Johnny; "peace and joy, that's what you and Minnie have got in your faces that makes you so—so different. And there's a peaceful look in Mr. Earnshaw's face, but his doesn't shine quite the way yours does. But how——?"

"It's like this, Johnny; God made us to love Him and serve Him, but we try to live our lives as *we* want and sometimes it seems to work and we think we are happy. But all the time we keep looking for something else and we know deep down inside it is because we are not really satisfied at all. We keep on measuring ourselves by other people and as God tells us that we have *all* sinned, what is the use of measuring ourselves by other sinners? When we find out what *God* thinks of sin, how He hates it and can have nothing at all to do with it, so that even *one* sin could keep us out of Heaven, then we begin to see that nothing we can do is any good at all. God loved His own dear Son with a love so great that we can never understand it, yet He sent Him down to earth to live as a Man among men and let Him die a horrible death to show us what a dreadful thing sin is and to pay for all the evil we had done and make us fit for Heaven. But we have to confess that we need Him and take the salvation He offers and serve Him in love and gratitude for His wonderful gift, then He gives us love in our hearts and peace in our faces and He shows us in many ways that He is real and that He cares for us."

"But," Johnny wavered, "how can I be *sure* He wants *me*?"

"Because God says so, Johnny; He says that it is for everyone who wants it. You want it, don't you?"

"Oh, I do! Whatever it is you've all got, I want it."

"Then ask Him for it. Kneel down here and just ask Him."

Obediently Johnny knelt, closed his eyes and bowed his head as he had so often seen Minnie do, and spoke softly.

"Please, God, I don't know much about You, but I like the people who love You a whole heap better than those who don't, so please won't You let me have what they've got, even though I'm not quite sure what it is? Maybe I could learn if You don't mind teaching me."

Mrs. Rosevear added, "Loving heavenly Father, take Johnny into Thy service and lead him in Thy way; forgive him all that he has done against Thee and make him clean through Thy blessed Son, our Lord Jesus Christ. Amen."

There was a brief silence, then Johnny said, "Thank You, God."

He stood up and looked at Mrs. Rosevear. "What I really came in about was Mum. When you told Dad you would pray about—about the drink—he was a bit disappointed you didn't tell him a prayer to say for himself. I told him Minnie's, but he didn't like that bit about dying. He said he wasn't fit to die yet, so I asked him if Mum was fit to die and he said he didn't know and I was to ask you."

"Tell me about your mother's death, Johnny. I've heard a little about it from the neighbours, but I would like to hear what you remember of it."

So Johnny told her.

"She knew she needed God's forgiveness," said Mrs. Rosevear; "she wanted to ask for it. She must have known about Him when she was young. She died asking Him to receive her soul. Yes, Johnny, I believe she was as fit as any of us can be. All we can do is to confess that we need God's forgiveness and accept it from Him; He is the only One Who can make us fit for Heaven."

Johnny drew a deep breath of relief. "And now I've got to learn about Him for myself, haven't I? You said I must serve Him, and I don't know how."

Mrs. Rosevear went to her bookshelf. "Minnie and I have Bibles of our own; if I give you my husband's Bible, will you promise to read it every day?"

Johnny's eyes shone; now that he could read, how gladly would he give the required promise. Apart from school books, this was the first book he had ever owned. He took it into his hands, opened it at random and read, slowly but correctly, "But beloved, be not ignorant of this one thing, that one day is with the Lord as a thousand years, and a thousand years as one day."

He lifted bewildered eyes to his friend's face. "Is it all as difficult as that? What does it mean?"

"Look, Johnny; my husband marked with red ink all the stories he used to tell Minnie; you read those first and they will teach you a great deal more about God and about Jesus. If you find things you don't understand, you can always ask me or Mr. Earnshaw or the minister, and I expect one of us will be able to help you. As for the verse you read, well, it seems to me that God's love is so great that every day that Jesus was down here on earth away from Him seemed like a thousand years and yet His patience is so great that He has already waited nearly two thousand years since Jesus died to gather in men, women and children for His family in Heaven."

Johnny nodded, remembering how long the days had seemed while the Rosevears were in Brighton and how quickly the time passed when he was happy. It was an idea that he could grasp, and he thanked his friend again for the Bible and turned homeward to tell his father all that had happened. Mr. Connell scratched his head in ever-increasing bewilderment, but a dim thought began to form in his mind that Johnny and his mother were in on something from which he was being left out. It was a very tiny seed, but seeds have within them the possibility of growth, and the hard ground of Mr. Connell's heart had been broken up by the tragedy of his wife's death.

Johnny next took his Bible to show to Mr. Earnshaw, who, on hearing that the lad had determined to be a Christian, gave him a hymn-book which had belonged to his son; he also suggested a series of readings and explained some of the words he would most often find.

Johnny found it all very interesting, though difficult. He was no coward and did not try to hide from others the change in his outlook, even when he had to bear the cutting contempt of one of the masters, the jeers of several of his school-mates and a little quiet bullying from others. When he could, he took refuge with the Rosevears or Mr. Earnshaw, and he formed the habit of meeting his father as he came from work. Mr. Connell, who was honestly trying to overcome his failing, would often come home with him and spend the evening listening with a new-found pride while Johnny read aloud; sometimes, with a touching humility, he would give his son all the money in his pockets except the price of a couple of drinks and tell him to go to the Rosevears and pray. He had a genuine respect for Mrs. Rosevear's prayers and usually came home sober.

One disastrous day, however, one of his mates won

a prize of some hundreds of pounds and celebrated by providing lavish free drinks for all his friends. When Johnny met his father, Mr. Connell was already too fuddled to listen to his entreaties and went off with the others to continue celebrations. Johnny set off at a run, only to remember that Mrs. Rosevear had taken Minnie to visit her brother and would not be home until fairly late. He slowed down, then stopped. For the first time since his conversion, doubts insinuated themselves into his mind. He had tried so hard; he had prayed—they had all prayed—yet here was Dad back on the booze and it was pay-day; that probably meant mighty little to eat all next week. It wasn't fair! Deep down inside, he was ashamed of this feeling but he was not yet ready to admit it, so he would not go to Mr. Earnshaw. Instead, he roamed moodily through a tangle of lanes leading to a little-used canal and wandered along its bank brooding. Two boys hidden in some rough bushes saw him, looked at each other in unspoken question and nodded.

"Hiya, Johnny!" sang out the elder.

Johnny started and turned round. "That you, Jim Bacon?"

"That's me," agreed Jim, parting the bushes and scrambling out, followed by his companion. They trotted up to Johnny with ingratiating grins and he waited quietly, wondering what two of his old gang could want with him now.

"You heard about Alfie Carter?" Jim blurted out.

Johnny widened his eyes and shook his head.

"Fine gang leader *he* turned out to be," declared Jim scornfully. "Got us mixed up in a fight with that gang in Shawberry Road and the police nabbed him knifing Tubby Lock. Reckon they'll put him away for six months at least!"

Johnny whistled thoughtfully. Jim again looked a question at the boy beside him, who nodded and offered Johnny a lump of stickjaw toffee. They watched him furtively until speech had obviously become a trifle difficult, then Jim said, "How about being boss of the gang again, Johnny?"

The other lad added eagerly, "We had heaps more fun when you was boss, Johnny! *You* never got us mixed up with the flatties! *You* never knifed no one!"

The flattery was balm to Johnny's misery. He forgot about his father, forgot the many times that he and the gang had run from angry neighbours and thought only of the thrill of giving orders to boys, several of whom were older and bigger than he was himself. . . . He was not the first to be tempted by the lure of power, nor would he be the last. He found himself feverishly planning gang activities that should prove to them all that he was a better leader than Alfie.

"And now," he ordered, "go get the rest of the gang—but mind, no more ratting, or I'm through!"

With fervent assurances of loyalty, they ran off. Johnny sat down and began thinking, somewhat uneasily. He measured the gang against the new standards he had learnt during the past months and realized that he would have to choose between loyalty to God and loyalty to the gang. For a time he tried to persuade himself that he could lead the gang and impose on them his own new sense of right and wrong but almost at once he knew it to be impossible. By the time Jim Bacon was back with eight others, Johnny's mind was in a turmoil of indecision. As they surrounded him, welcoming him back to the leadership, he closed his eyes for a second and whispered,

"Please, God, help me!"

Chapter 6

THE GANG

THE first-comers were still talking volubly when the last two of the gang ran up, one, George Harris, shouting triumphantly, "Look what I've got!"

The others came round him curiously and he opened his jacket to show a small black kitten whose flattened-back ears and terrified eyes showed that it had been none too well treated.

"What you going to do with that?" inquired Johnny.

"Drown it in the canal, of course," George replied. Johnny stiffened.

"You like drowning kittens?"

"Rather!" George gloated. "It ain't 'alf funny watching 'em struggle!"

Johnny looked round him. "All those who want to help drown that kitten, hands up."

George shot up his hand, so did five others, followed hesitatingly by a seventh lad.

"Anyone against?" inquired Johnny casually. Jim Bacon put up his hand, grumbling, "I *like* kittens." Two others followed, then three more. Johnny looked at the last boy.

"You put up your hand just now for drowning it. Make up your mind!"

Sandy kicked a pebble into the canal. "*I* like kittens, too," he admitted. "I only put up my hand because the others did."

Johnny reached out his hand for the kitten, which George unsuspectingly handed over. He stroked it and tickled its ears and the little cat, sensing that it was in friendly hands, ventured a faint purr. His glance flicked right and left as he swiftly planned. Suddenly Johnny sprinted down the tow-path to the lock-keeper's cottage, thrust the kitten through the open window with a breathless "Look after it for a few minutes, please!" and turned back to face the pursuing gang.

"Fight you for it, George Harris!" he defied. "All of you if I must—but we don't all like drowning kittens!"

George didn't stop to argue; furious, he hit out, but Johnny ducked neatly and, as he hit back, noted with the tail of his eye that the gang were evenly divided and that six fights were raging along the tow-path. All were seasoned fighters and soon there were black eyes and bleeding noses, cut lips and at least one torn jacket. Johnny remembered thankfully that he had on his old suit; only that morning Mrs. Rosevear had noticed a missing button and a torn pocket and had insisted he should change and give her his new suit to mend.

Johnny was thinking coolly yet rapidly; George was still in too furious a temper to fight with his usual skill. Suddenly Johnny saw his chance and with one blow to the unguarded chin sent George reeling into the canal. As if at a signal, all the other fights stopped and the boys gathered round to watch him, laughing and jeering at first, until Jim Bacon called out uneasily,

"He can't swim—he's—drowning!"

It was true. Fury had given way to panic for although the canal was not deep it was slippery with mud and he could not get to his feet. Johnny jumped in, grabbed one flailing arm and dragged him towards the bank, where the others helped to haul them both out. George gave his rescuer one ugly look, then turned homeward, muttering under his breath what he meant to do to Johnny when he got the chance. The others watched him go, then looked curiously at Johnny. One soon made up his mind.

"All that fuss about a kitten!" he said, contemptuously turned his back on them and struck off across the lock gates, followed by two others. Don Marshall and Micky Green joined Johnny's supporters. Don looked at Micky, his special chum, and spoke for both of them.

"I call that rotten, after you hauled him out. Reckon you saved his life. We're sorry about the kitten. O.K.?"

Johnny nodded rather absently; he was still thinking hard. Suddenly he made up his mind.

"I don't think I can be gang leader, after all. I—you see——" He floundered to a stop. This was the first time he had had to confess to the gang his new loyalty and he had all a normal boy's dread of ridicule.

"Well, come on, cough it up, Johnny," said Bert Harper impatiently.

For the first time it came home to Johnny that there is more than one kind of cowardice. Physical courage he never had lacked but something more than physical courage was needed now. With a wordless prayer for help, he began.

"Before, when I was gang leader, I didn't care what we did so long as we got away with it. Now—well, it just doesn't seem smart any longer to lie and cheat and steal and swear and swap dirty stories and have gang fights over nothing except just to find out who's strongest——"

"Softy!" sneered Bert Harper witheringly. "Johnny Nursie! Johnny's girl-friend's been preaching to him!"

Johnny's fist shot out. Sneers for himself he had expected and been prepared to meet; sneers at Minnie caught him off his guard. At once the gang made a ring to enjoy the fight. Bert was the bigger and heavier but Johnny was quicker on his feet and landed two blows for every one he received. Bert, finding that he was getting the worst of it, watched his opportunity, hooked his foot round Johnny's ankle and tripped him up; his head hit a large stone and he lay still. Immediately the gang scattered. The lock-keeper, who had been watching with some interest since the arrival of the kitten, now hurried out; by the time he reached him, Johnny had opened his eyes and was trying to sit up.

The lock-keeper, a kindly man, helped him back to the cottage and told him to lie down while he made a cup of tea. The little black kitten crept up trustfully and was soon curled in a soft ball on Johnny's lap. When the lock-keeper came in with the tea, he poured it a saucer of milk, which Johnny held until it had lapped up every drop and had licked its nose and whiskers; only then would he take his cup of tea. A few questions and the lock-keeper had the whole story.

"Anyone trying to drown a kitten anywhere round here is going to wish he'd never been born!" he prophesied darkly.

Johnny, chuckling, thanked him and stood up to go.

"Sure you'll be all right?" asked his new friend.

"Quite sure," replied Johnny confidently, and, tucking the kitten inside his jacket, he set off for home. He kept a sharp look-out for the gang but they, not sure how badly he was hurt, kept in hiding. George had been sent to bed in disgrace for coming home wet through—and that also he set down against Johnny.

It was fairly late now and there was a light in the Rosevears' window, so Johnny knocked and asked, "Oh, Mrs. Rosevear, would Minnie like a kitten?"

Mrs. Rosevear looked at him. "Oh, Johnny," she returned sorrowfully, "you've been fighting!"

The eagerness died out of the lad's face; thinking only of offering the kitten, he had forgotten his appearance. He studied her face anxiously, but saw no anger—only grief and pity; she drew him in, helped him wash away some of the signs of battle and put something soothing on his bruises. Meanwhile Minnie welcomed the kitten joyfully, took it on her lap and petted it until it purred as though it thought itself in a cat's paradise.

Mrs. Rosevear questioned Johnny gently about the fight and praised him warmly for saving the kitten. Then came the question.

"But how was it you were not with your father?"

Johnny's downcast face answered for him. Mrs. Rosevear put the final stitches into a jacket seam, finished it off neatly, then laid aside her mending basket and put on her hat and coat.

"You stay here with Minnie," she said, "and I'll go and look for your father. I'm told one of the men round here has won some big prize or other and I can guess what that means."

Friendly little Mrs. Rosevear already knew many of her neighbours; now she went round to one or two whose husbands haunted the local pubs and soon she had the information she wanted—the men were all in the Bunch of Grapes. She marched along there, tremulous but determined, and was guided in her quest by that raucous din which the very drunk mistake for music. She pushed open the door, gasped at the mingled reek of drink and tobacco, but peered into the blaze of light, dazzling after the dark streets, until she saw Mr. Connell. The singing had died down a little as some of those nearest the door recognized her; one or two shouted a greeting, and when Mr. Connell heard her name he turned and faced her. His jaw dropped and he made a futile attempt to hide behind the others, but she went straight to him, saying,

"I hope you'll come home to Johnny now, Mr. Connell; he needs you—and I'm thinking you need him!"

One or two swore at her for a spoil-sport, others guffawed and shouted coarse jests that made her cheeks burn, but she stood her ground. Mr. Connell held up his hand with an attempt at dignity, saying,

"Mushn't shpeak like that to a lady—none of 'ush in fit shtate to shpeak to lady!"

"I hope you're ashamed of yourself," she said quietly. The prize-winner broke in at this.

"Nothing to be 'shamed of, ma'am—only natural shelebrate—'ave one on me—any friend of my mate ish friend of mine."

Mrs. Rosevear ignored him and continued to look appealingly at Mr. Connell, who grew more and more uneasy and even made an uncertain move towards her; his entertainer, resenting this as a slight to his hospitality, grasped his arm, saying with an oath,

"You leave here at closing time and not a minute before!"

Others took sides, and almost at once a quarrel developed into a fight and the publican, concerned for his licence, called out, "No fights here, gentlemen!" and thrust the combatants towards the street. Some of their more sober mates dragged them apart and tried to steer them home. Mrs. Rosevear saw her opportunity and seized it.

"Come along now," she coaxed, taking Mr. Connell's arm. He looked at her unhappily, taking a step or two.

"No fit shtate—walk with a lady," he muttered.

"Well," she retorted as he lurched, "seemingly you're in no fit state to walk without me, either, so make your choice!"

He came at that, trying very hard to walk steadily but making a poor show at it. He was a good six inches taller than she and strongly built; as they came out of the door he slipped from her grasp and collapsed on the pavement outside. She looked at him despairingly, for she had all the law-abiding citizen's horror of public drunkenness with its attendant danger of getting mixed up with the police. Now, however, help came from an unexpected quarter. Out of the shadows came the woman, Mrs. McGinnis, who had directed her to the Bunch of Grapes.

"I'll 'elp yer get 'im 'ome, dearie," she volunteered. "Now then, you, up yer gets!"

She was a powerfully-built woman, and between them they got Mr. Connell to his feet and steered him down the road. To Mrs. Rosevear, every step of the journey home was a nightmare of horror and shame, but she would not give up her self-appointed task, not even when for the third time he slipped to the ground and a policeman came up with an authoritative, "What's going on here?"

Mrs. Rosevear looked up with anguished appeal. "Oh please, officer," she pleaded, "leave him to us! We'll get him home!"

"You his wife?" he inquired.

"No, indeed!" she replied thankfully.

"Just a neighbour," put in her helper. "She's been a good friend to Johnny and I bet it's for Johnny's sake she's come out to get his Daddy home."

The policeman allowed them to go on and even followed a little way in case traffic at the main road proved awkward. The worst humiliation of the evening, however, came when they reached their own road. One of Johnny's gang had scouted round to try and find out how badly he was hurt; passing the Rosevears' window he saw Johnny with Minnie, playing with the kitten, and had gathered several of the gang to show that they need fear nothing on his account. All were on the spot when Mr. Connell and his escort staggered into the street, and their hoots of derision called most of the neighbours to doors and windows to enjoy the sight. Just as they reached his front door, the experienced Mrs. McGinnis called suddenly,

"Look out! He's going to be sick!" She held on with the skill of long practice; Mrs. Rosevear shuddered and did her best. Johnny, hearing the jeers and laughter outside, came to help and together they got him into his bed, Mrs. Rosevear now frankly weeping to think that anyone could find amusement in such a spectacle. Presently Mrs. McGinnis said,

"'E'll be all right when 'e's slep' it off, duck. Now, Johnny, you better put yourself to bed, and you'd best get back now and look after Minnie, Mrs. Rosevear. Shall I come in and make you a cup of tea?"

Mrs. Rosevear hesitated, but, suspecting that her neighbour was both cold and tired, she took her into the house and set a good meal on the table, eating what she could herself to encourage her guest. Presently Mrs. McGinnis sat back replete.

"Bless yer kind 'eart," she said gratefully, "I know why you done that. There ain't much I can do for you, but if you want to keep Johnny's Dad out of mischief, I'll keep an eye on 'im same as I does on my old man—not that it's much good in 'is case; 'e's too far gorn. But Johnny's Dad ain't that bad yet, and with you and me and Johnny to 'elp 'im, maybe 'e'll give it up."

Mrs. Rosevear replied softly but clearly, "You and I, Johnny and Minnie—and God."

Mrs. McGinnis stared. "What's God got to do with it?"

"Only God can give Mr. Connell strength to fight against temptation. We are all praying for him; would you like us to pray for your husband, too?"

"If you think it'll do any good," returned Mrs. McGinnis doubtfully. She knew little about God, or about prayer either, but was prepared to try anything once. They knelt together and Mrs. Rosevear poured out her overburdened heart to God. She rose with a new strength and resolution, and even Mrs. McGinnis had a more peaceful face as she turned to the door.

Mrs. Rosevear impulsively kissed her good-bye. The hard, bitter face softened and lit up, and with a pang of sympathy her new friend realized that not so very long ago Mrs. McGinnis had been a pretty girl. The poor woman went back comforted to her squalid and lonely room; she even glanced round and planned how to make it look a bit more respectable just in case—she hardly dared venture to hope—but in case prayer *could* change things.

Chapter 7

MORNING AFTER

IT was a pleasant October morning, but Mr. Connell, waking with a throbbing head and a foul taste in his mouth, lay and worried about what he could remember of the previous night. There were things he couldn't remember—how he got home, for instance, and how, drunk as he must have been, he had contrived to put himself to bed and fold his clothes neatly over the back of the chair.

"Johnny," he called presently. Johnny appeared almost at once with a steaming cup of strong coffee which his father accepted gratefully, casting furtive glances at his son as he sipped.

"Johnny," he ventured at last, "what happened last night?"

"Mrs. Rosevear and Mrs. McGinnis brought you home and put you to bed."

Mr. Connell's jaw dropped and he hastily put down his cup, incredulity slowly giving way to dismay.

"Did—did she say anything—about me?"

"She cried," Johnny answered briefly. Mr. Connell took up his cup, sipped and pondered.

"What'll I do now, Johnny?"

Johnny shrugged. How should he know? Mr. Connell finished his coffee, glanced at the clock and got up, groaning at the throbbing of his head. He washed, dressed and hurried off to work. Johnny reluctantly got ready for school, dreading the taunts that he expected. However, the fried fish shop at the corner proved to be on fire and in the excitement last night was forgotten. After school he met his father and was thankful to find him still very subdued; he even suggested going round to apologize, and Johnny brightened up and encouraged him. As he preferred to do it alone, Johnny went in to get the meal ready. Mr. Connell knocked at his neighbour's door, took off his cap and stood twisting it round and round. When the door opened he stole a glance at Mrs. Rosevear's face and began,

"I'm that sorry and ashamed, ma'am, I don't know what to say." The cap twisted more rapidly and he looked so absurdly like a scolded child that she smiled involuntarily.

"If you never spoke to me again, I'm sure I couldn't blame you," he went on, but looking up again he caught the smile, brightened and ventured,

"If you'd help me try again—I've no confidence in myself—not after last night. I thought I was doing so well, too!"

"And so you were," she assured him warmly, "but good resolutions aren't enough. Look now, have your supper, for I'm sure you need it, then let Johnny come in and sit with Minnie and you come round with me to our minister, Mr. Venner. I don't feel I can talk to you like he could, and you met him at your wife's funeral, so it's not like going to a stranger. Will you do it?"

Mr. Connell hesitated, feeling vaguely that he had reached cross-roads in his life, then he straightened up and looked her straight in the eyes.

"I'll come, ma'am, and thank you kindly."

When Johnny understood what was planned, he edged up bashfully and squeezed his father's arm. He didn't venture to say anything but his look was enough; he and Minnie beamed at each other in joyful expectation.

"I'm sure it's going to be all right!" proclaimed Minnie, then, too shy to speak of prayer about something that meant so much to Johnny, she picked up the kitten and buried her face in its soft fur while her loving little heart put up a petition that was no less fervent for being silent.

Meanwhile the other two had arrived at the Manse. Mrs. Venner, who had heard a little of the story, made her own estimate of the importance of the visit and showed them straight into her husband's study. He, too, after one look at Mr. Connell's face, pushed aside his unfinished sermon, settled his visitors in comfortable fireside chairs and waited in expectant, understanding silence while Mr. Connell opened his mouth, shut it again and gazed appealingly from one to the other. Mrs. Rosevear smiled encouragingly and began,

"It's like this, Mr. Venner; ever since Mrs. Connell died he's been trying real hard to give up the drink but yesterday one of his mates won a lot of money and stood treat to celebrate and—well——"

Mr. Venner nodded. "Temptation proved too strong. Now you feel you need help. But is drink your *only* reason for needing help?"

Mr. Connell considered this uneasily. "Well, no, sir. I don't know just what is wrong, but when Sally died and Johnny tried to teach me that prayer, I knew I wasn't fit to die. I don't think I'm any worse than most folk, but—well—I didn't fancy having to explain away some of the things I done. I didn't look after Sally right, for one thing, and it seems as if I've left other people to look after me own son. And there's other things——"

"We'll leave the other things just now," interposed Mr. Venner, "and look at what you have just said. Would it be any defence in an English law court if you said, 'I have committed a murder, but apart from that I am no worse than other men'?"

Mr. Connell looked startled and a little indignant. "*I* ain't done no murders," he protested.

"No, but would it be any defence?"

"Why, no, sir; of course not."

"Jesus said that the two greatest commandments are to love God with all there is of you and to love others—*all* others—as much as you love yourself. Have you done that?"

Again Mr. Connell pondered, then admitted, "No, sir."

"And if you have broken the two greatest commandments, does it not prove you guilty of the two greatest sins?"

"I suppose so, sir, if you put it like that."

"Everything else is included in that, so are you not admitting that you see your need of God's forgiveness?"

"When you put it that way, sir, I can't get away from it, can I?"

"But because God is a perfectly holy God, He can never just *forgive* sin. Someone must pay the price, and because He is also a perfectly loving God, He sent His own beloved son to live as a Man among men, to show what absolute purity, truth and love mean, then, when that perfect life deserved to end by going back in triumph to the Heaven that He was perfectly fit to enter, God let Him die for us—to pay our debt. All He asks of you now is to confess that you need forgiveness, to accept the forgiveness He offers and to show your gratitude by changing sides from serving His enemies to serving Him. Then He promises all the power we need to fight loyally; in addition, He offers all eternity with Him, free from everything that can hurt or distress us and surrounded for ever by such happiness in His presence as we cannot even imagine."

"He offers that, to *me*?" It seemed too good to be true.

"All that, and more, to you. Will you take it?"

"I will indeed, sir. It's more than I can rightly take in just at first. Will you give me a minute or two to think it out and try to understand?"

They watched in sympathetic silence while unaccustomed thoughts and emotions worked through his mind. Presently he spoke again.

"I bin remembering a Froggie we took prisoner in the war—Frenchman from Alsace, Jacques, I think his name was. He fell in love with a German girl, served in the German army to please her. When we captured 'im, 'is papers showed 'e was a Frenchy, see? 'E tells us 'ow it all come about, but a French officer asked if no one ever told 'im 'e was French and 'e admitted they 'ad but 'e 'adn't took no notice. Well, 'e stood trial and they shot 'im for a traitor. Ain't that a bit like me? I bin told more than once about coming in on God's side but I chose the devil's side. Well now, as I see it, 'stead of taking me out and shooting me as a traitor, God is saying I can join His army now and He'll trust me to serve Him true and loyal. That right, sir?"

"Yes," agreed Mr. Venner. "That man may have been a good soldier and well thought of by his friends, but that was of no use to him when his own people captured him. Many people think themselves perfectly all right because they are like those around them and never realize that they are fighting on the wrong side. They are quite content where they are and will bitterly resent the suggestion that they need to change their whole outlook, but at present the whole world is enemy-occupied territory and when the true King comes back, the test will be whether you joined the Resistance and fought for Him in His absence or whether you collaborated with the enemy."

"Right, sir," declared Mr. Connell. "Will you put down my name as joining the Resistance from now on?"

"Gladly," replied the minister, shaking hands heartily. "May I strongly recommend daily Bible reading and prayer? Have you a Bible, by the way?"

Mr. Connell shook his head and Mr. Venner leaned over to his book-shelves and took out three books.

"I was given a number of these," he explained, "to give away where I thought they might be of use. This is the new American version of the Bible, and while I feel it is not a perfect rendering, it is in modern English, which you will find easier to understand than the Authorized Version, many of whose words have completely changed their meaning in the last few generations. I hope that you will come regularly to church, too, for that is a great help."

"You tell me when and I'll be there," replied Mr. Connell earnestly. "If God's trusting me to serve Him true and loyal then I'll *serve* Him true and loyal, and I won't dodge none of my parades."

Mr. Venner took a sheet of paper and wrote rapidly. "Sunday there is morning service at eleven, evening service at six-thirty. At three there is Sunday School, which I should like Johnny to attend. On Monday evenings at eight there is the Men's Fellowship, where you would get to know some of your fellow-Christians. Wednesday evening at eight we meet for prayer and praise and to study all that is meant by being a Christian. On Friday evening at eight there is a Youth Club where Johnny could meet youngsters between ten and fifteen, after which they move up into Junior Church."

Mr. Connell studied his paper and stood up. "Right, sir," he said; "I'll be seeing you on Sunday at eleven then—and—thank you for the books—and everything."

He said little on the way back, but when he went in to fetch Johnny home he said humbly,

"Johnny, my boy, your Daddy's enlisted tonight under your Captain, and I'll try to be a better father to you than I've ever been."

Minnie astonished them all by sliding off her chair and hopping excitedly across the room to fling her arms round Mr. Connell, exulting,

"We prayed! We prayed! Didn't we, Mummie? Ever since Johnny's mother died, we prayed that you would learn to love him like my Mummie loves me! And you will now, won't you?"

Mrs. McGinnis, who had drifted along with a vague hope of hearing more about prayer, reached the window at this moment and looked in, at first with a dull disappointment that Mrs. Rosevear was not free; then she realized who were the visitors and, remembering her neighbour as he had looked only the night before, she gasped, amazed that he should now look so perfectly at home. She hung about until Johnny and his father came out, when she confronted them as if by accident. Mr. Connell looked somewhat embarrassed, but held out his hand and thanked her for her help the previous night, adding quietly,

"You'll never have that to do again, I promise you."

She drew still nearer, peering into his face.

"Was it"—she hesitated—"like she said? Was it—prayer—what done it, mate?"

"Yes, I think it must have been."

"Then—I done *you* a good turn last night, mate. Will yer—will yer say a prayer for my old man?"

Both Mr. Connell and Johnny gladly promised.

That night, in her lonely room, Mrs. McGinnis said very softly,

"Please, God, keep my old man off the drink." Then with a strange new peace in her heart, she fell asleep.

Chapter 8

SHOWING HIS COLOURS

MR. CONNELL woke early the next morning and, hearing movement in Johnny's room, went in to find Johnny climbing back into bed with his Bible. He suggested that Johnny should read aloud while he followed in his own new Bible. Johnny, who was learning to find his way fairly easily, opened both Bibles at Mark, Chapter 14, and began to read. Gripped by the story, Mr. Connell soon lost his own place and listened quietly until Johnny read,

"And they all forsook Him and fled."

"What, *all* of them?" he interrupted.

"That's what it says here," Johnny replied uncertainly. "What does yours say, then?"

His father found the place and read aloud,

"'And they all forsook Him and fled.' Well, but wasn't they all saying they wouldn't rat, not if they was to die for it?"

Johnny thought a moment, then said slowly,

"Mrs. Rosevear told me there was things they couldn't do until after Jesus died and came alive again to give them the power."

Mr. Connell, slightly deflated, said,

"Oh—like I couldn't keep off the drink when I

thought I could?" Then, wistfully, "Johnny, you're *sure* I shall be able to now?"

Desperately Johnny seized his arm.

"Dad, you've *got* to believe that! What's the use of enlisting under a new Captain and even *thinking* of deserting back to the enemy? What you got to do is learn the drill and be a better soldier each day."

Mr. Connell chuckled suddenly. "Johnny, my boy, you and me we're a couple of raw recruits! We'll have Mrs. Rosevear for sergeant and the minister can be Lootenant Venner! The thing to do, Johnny, is not to shirk our drill."

They finished the chapter and Mr. Connell observed thoughtfully,

"Johnny, Jesus *knew* they was going to rat on Him, but He went through with it just the same. Now that's what I call courage."

Mr. Connell, shy at the thought of going to church on his own, or even with Johnny, who was eager to come, sent him next door to ask whether they might all go together, but, once dressed in his best suit and on his way, he quietly took charge, wheeled Minnie's chair, lifted it into the church hall and carried the child to her favourite seat, well up towards the front. He found himself enjoying the simple service, especially that part of it which Mr. Venner addressed to the children in the front rows, and sang the hymns in a way that showed Mrs. Rosevear whence Johnny had inherited his quick ear for a tune. When collection time came he ransacked his pockets, while his knitted brows suggested that a little mental arithmetic was going on. Finally he selected and dropped in a half-crown and quietly pushed a sixpence into Johnny's hand. As they came away he asked many questions—when were collections taken, for what purpose, how much was it right to give? To this Mrs. Rosevear replied that it was left to the conscience of each, but that God's law for his people of Israel had been one shilling in every ten, and after that duty, anything extra they chose to give out of love, and that He had promised a special blessing to those who obeyed.

"And do all church people do that?"

"Very few," she confessed. "That is why so many churches try to raise money by jumble sales, socials and all sorts of other activities."

He stopped and looked at her. "And—you?"

"I give my tenth," she told him, reddening slightly.

He moved forward again, deep in thought, but said no more until they were home. As he said good-bye, he added,

"This wants thinking out, ma'am; I must see my way."

As they ate, Mr. Connell set to work with pencil and paper. Presently he sat back and looked thoughtfully at Johnny.

"Seems to me," he observed, "I bin spending about three quid a week on beer, fags, pools and the dogs and then grousing because I never had no money at the end of the week. I'm cutting that right out. That means I can give my tenth and still have money in hand. How about regular pocket money for you?"

Johnny's face lit up. "Oh, Dad!" he cried joyfully.

His father looked him over.

"It don't do that new suit of yours any good to wear it all the time and you're fair bursting out o' the seams of your old one. Another new suit each?"

Johnny fidgeted with a box of matches.

"Yes, Dad, that would be fine," he agreed, but he had not yet reached the age when clothes meant very much to him and there was obviously some other thought in his mind. Mr. Connell waited a while, puzzled, then took away the matches, put his hand under Johnny's chin, tilted his face and said,

"Out with it, son!"

Johnny grinned; this new understanding and interest made him feel wanted and important. Haltingly at first, then more and more eagerly, he told his father about the visit to Brighton when he had seen Mrs. Rosevear's cousin carving a boat; he showed the one he had been given and the copy he was attempting, and at last spoke of Mr. Earnshaw's inquiries about wood-carving classes. There was a really good one, quite near, only—only there were fees to be paid, tools and wood to be bought. Mr. Connell looked at Johnny's work with real interest. His own carpentry had always been of the more practical kind but he recognized at once that not only had Johnny inherited aptitude, but the boat, crude and amateurish as it was, held a suggestion of beauty and grace that gave promise of something beyond routine work.

"Yes, my lad, you shall have your chance. I tell you straight, that's better than I could have done at your age!"

The only adequate way in which Johnny could express his feelings was to turn three somersaults in succession!

When it was time for Johnny to go to Sunday School Mr. Connell went with him to the church and lingered at the door so wistfully that Mr. Venner, recognizing him and coming over for a chat, called one of the bigger boys and suggested that they should go into the deacons' vestry and have a class of their own. The lad looked startled but interested and marched his pupil off willingly enough, reappearing at the end of the hour triumphant to show that Mr. Connell could now recite the Lord's Prayer.

After evening church, Mr. Venner introduced two of the Men's Fellowship, while Mr. Earnshaw, recognizing Johnny, also came over and spoke. Mr. Connell managed a few awkward but sincere words of thanks for his friendship to Johnny.

"He's worth it!" replied Mr. Earnshaw cordially and father and son glowed with pleasure.

Work next day brought its problems. The shop steward was trying to persuade the men to strike for higher pay. The management, already paying the highest wages they could without increasing their selling prices, had refused to consider an increase, and on this Monday morning Stanton was working his way round, whispering his propaganda to all those whom he knew he could most easily influence. Among these he had mentally numbered Mr. Connell and swaggering up he clapped him on the shoulder with a confident,

"I know we can count on *you*!"

Mr. Connell looked at him thoughtfully. Only a few days back, he knew, he would have agreed at once; now he was not so sure. To go out on strike would be a poor return for the kindness they had shown him when his wife died. He remembered also that in his last job the wages had not been so good, nor was there a staff canteen. Another point occurred to him—strike pay would be far less than his pay-packet, and would upset the plans that he and Johnny had so joyfully made.

"No, Mr. Stanton," he stated, clearly and decidedly, "I'm not interested in strike action, thank you."

Several of his work-mates heard and gathered round, some calling him "blackleg", some agreeing with him, but one man with a jeer and an oath cried,

"Saw 'im comin' out o' church last night; what's the betting old Connell's got religion?"

Connell whitened, then flushed. He would certainly never have chosen this way to publish his change of heart but, since the challenge was out, he must answer it.

"If you mean that I had the sense to see I was

serving a bad master and have changed to a better One, you're right," he retorted. There was a burst of laughter, catcalls and, from Stanton, a sneering,

"Religion! The opium of the people! Pie in the sky by and by!"

Others, hearing the dispute, gathered round. The foreman, recognizing a tense situation and not anxious to be the spark to touch off an explosion, quietly walked round the corner. Connell looked at the ring of faces and an idea came to him; raising his voice, he cried,

"Listen, you chaps; you don't want to strike with the cold weather coming on and the missis and the kids going short and nothing in the kitty for Christmas; you forget all this strike talk for six months and at the end of it"—he swung round and pointed at Stanton, whom he knew to be a heavy drinker—"at the end of six months, I challenge you to say which of us looks most as if he'd been fed on 'the opium of the people'!"

There was a burst of more friendly laughter, and one man called out,

"I call that a sporting offer! I'll lay a quid on Connell; any takers?"

There was more laughter at this and bet after bet was made. Stanton, intelligent enough to recognize the changed atmosphere, assumed a geniality he was far from feeling and went to his bench. Others followed and the foreman reported to the manager that Connell seemed to have a trick of handling men and might be worth watching for promotion. His work-mates, however, began watching him for other reasons; those who had bet against him lost no chance of trying to tempt him back to the drink, while others gave rough encouragement or furtively watched all that he did. Uneasily conscious of this, he talked the whole thing over with Mr. Venner, who pointed out to him the verses in Paul's letter to the Romans, "If thou shalt confess with thy mouth Jesus as Lord and shalt believe in thine heart that God hath raised Him from the dead, thou shalt be saved, for with the heart man believeth unto righteousness; and with the mouth confession is made unto salvation." "This is one point," he added, "where my comparison with the Resistance Movement breaks down; God wants soldiers who love Him enough to confess publicly that they are His."

"So I done the right thing without knowing it," he marvelled. "I can see I shall have to get to know King's Regulations a lot better; I wouldn't have needed to come bothering you if I'd knowed that bit was there."

"Never think you are 'bothering' me when you bring me your problems," Mr. Venner countered swiftly; "I am here to help you and God has given us the church that we may help each other."

"Help each other?" queried Mr. Connell; "how could *I* help anyone?"

"Have you never heard the Salvation Army motto, 'Saved to Serve'?" Mr. Venner replied. "You have been a soldier and could help our Life Boys with their drill; you are a carpenter and could run a carpentry class for any who were interested. Later, when you know your Bible better, I hope you will take a Sunday School class; we need more teachers."

His visitor looked interested but a trifle taken aback and rose to go. Mr. Venner wisely said no more but left him to think it out for himself. More harm than good may be done by too much haste at the beginning; it is better to lay the foundations well before trying to build on them. The remark about carpentry had, however, put an idea into Mr. Connell's head and he hurried home to Johnny and put it before him.

"How would it be if you and me made Minnie a dolls' house for Christmas?"

Johnny's eyes widened. "Well, if that ain't funny! Last time I took Minnie to that little park in Marlow Lane there was a dolls' house in that big toyshop just before you get to it and she made me stop so she could look at it. The whole front opened like a cupboard and you could see all the rooms and the furniture and little dolls and she thought it was just about perfect! Then she asked what it cost and the ticket said twenty-five pounds so she just said, 'Come on, Johnny, let's get on to the park'."

"Wonder if it's still there? Tell you what, Johnny, let's go and look."

The dolls' house was still in the window and Mr. Connell looked it over with a professional eye.

"I reckon I could make one pretty near as good for

twenty-five shillings," he declared, "and we could make most of the furniture out of bits and pieces. Let's do it, Johnny, shall we?"

Johnny beamed his approval. A voice behind them said wistfully,

"I suppose you couldn't manage two while you're about it? My little girl's mad for one but I can't afford twenty-five pounds and I'm an absolute fool with tools. I could manage seven or eight pounds."

Johnny and his father looked at the speaker, then at each other; the same thought was in both minds—it would mean a lot of hard work to make and furnish *two* dolls' houses before Christmas. They looked again into two pleading brown eyes and suddenly they knew that they must do it. The stranger's face fairly shone; as they exchanged addresses, he added,

"Any night after eight—Rose goes to bed at eight and I want it to be a surprise. Roffen's the name."

Mr. Connell replied, "Any Tuesday, Thursday or Saturday after seven you may care to come along and see how it's shaping; you might like yours a bit different."

They set off for home with rather thoughtful faces but soon Mr. Connell brightened.

"Guess I'm going to have enough on my hands to keep me out of mischief!" he grinned. "I reckon it's like what that youngster taught me that first afternoon you went to Sunday School—'Lead us not into temptation but deliver us from evil'. If He's leading me to use my time for something better than the pub and the dogs and all that, then I say, Thank You, Lord!"

Johnny said nothing, but the expression of joyful affection on his face was answer enough.

Chapter 9

MRS. ROSEVEAR IS LONELY

JOHNNY had never been so happy in his life; the new comradeship with his father had transformed his home; thanks to Mr. Earnshaw he was doing quite well at school, and spare time was divided between the Rosevears, wood-carving classes, church and the dolls' houses until there seemed scarcely hours enough in the day for all he wanted to do. It was not long before Mr. Roffen came to see how his dolls' house was getting on and to offer a suggestion.

"I'm in wholesale tailoring and have only to ask for bundles of pieces left over when cutting out; if you can give me a few measurements to guide me, I can make carpets for the floors, curtains for the windows, bedclothes—all that sort of thing—and I'd be glad to make a set for yours as well. There isn't much to do once Rose goes to bed."

"Just the two of you?" inquired Mr. Connell sympathetically.

"My wife's in hospital and may not be out until Christmas; I have to be father and mother to Rose just now."

"I'm sorry; hope she makes it by Christmas. Now about measurements—I can give you floor area for carpets, and window sizes, but I want to finish the houses before I start fiddling with furniture."

Somewhat diffidently he produced a book of out-of-date wallpaper begged from a builder he knew, explaining that he meant to paper the walls; Mr. Roffen was delighted and together they chose the pattern for each room and made duplicate notes so that fabrics might match papers everywhere.

Not long after this, the doctor visited Minnie one morning. As he walked into the room, the kitten crouched, darted at his shoe-lace and fled back to Minnie's couch. The doctor laughed and bent to stroke the little thing, which purred loudly and rubbed its head against his hand.

"So you have a kitten now, have you? I expect you have great games together?"

Minnie laughed happily. "Oh yes, he's such company when Mother is out!"

The doctor undid the bandages and examined her leg carefully.

"Yes," he said thoughtfully, "as I expected. Minnie, how would you like to run about like other little girls?"

She caught her breath and looked up at him eagerly. He turned to Mrs. Rosevear.

"We must get her away to hospital, fit an artificial foot and teach her how to use it, and thanks to her swimming and the kitten I believe we can get it all done in time for her to be home for Christmas!"

There were tears in Mrs. Rosevear's eyes as she softly exclaimed,

"Thank God! Oh, thank God! Minnie has been as good as gold and *so* patient and Johnny next door has been a great help—he gave her the kitten, too—but it is only natural that she feels being kept in so much and not doing all the things other children can do."

Arrangements were soon completed. Minnie clung to her mother when the time for parting came, but she was eager to walk again and faced bravely all the unpleasant part that she knew could not be avoided. She had always been a friendly little soul and took a great interest in the other children in her ward, but if she suffered little from loneliness, Mrs. Rosevear found the parting less easy to bear. She was allowed to visit the hospital three days a week and always took Minnie some home-made treat to share with the others in the ward; she had her work and her church to take up much of her time, but there were still hours that hung heavily and she looked round for occupation. The Connells spent an evening with her, other neighbours called in for an hour or two when they had time, then she suggested to Mr. Connell that she should overhaul his wardrobe and Johnny's. He brightened, then looked thoughtful and scratched his head uneasily.

"Ma'am," he said hesitantly, "they do say that a woman can't keep a secret; now would that be true, do you think?"

"Certainly not," she replied indignantly. "I have met men who were far worse gossips than any woman!"

He looked relieved and led the way into his front

room. At once Mrs. Rosevear saw two dolls' houses, one in each fireside alcove, and with a little cry of delight she went to the nearest and studied it eagerly. It was finished and painted to look like golden-brown brick with a tiled roof made of grey-green linoleum, each tile glued into position. There were golden-brown chimney-stacks with little brown chimneys, and tiny gutters with drain-pipes running down from them. The front and back of the house opened on hinges to show all the rooms, which were papered and carpeted except for a tiled bathroom and kitchen. A tiny staircase had both carpet and stair-rods. Each window was curtained and the drawing-room had a pelmet and satin curtains which could be drawn across the windows. There was as yet no furniture, but a table obviously meant for the dining-room stood with six chairs, complete except for their seats, on the work-bench. Suddenly Mrs. Rosevear gave a little excited exclamation.

"I have three little wooden dolls in a cupboard; they were my mother's when she was a child—Dutch dolls she said they were, and I am sure they are just the size for this house. You are making one of these for Minnie, aren't you? That's why you want me to keep it secret! I could dress them in time for Christmas—their clothes are old and faded."

Mr. Connell admitted that one was for Minnie and added diffidently,

"I suppose you couldn't let me see those dolls? I am making the other house for a little girl whose mother is in hospital and I might be able to make her a set of dolls as well."

"Why, of course! I'll fetch them now." And off she whisked, to return a few minutes later with three little jointed wooden dolls with painted hair and faces. Mr. Connell examined them with interest, for they are hardly ever seen now, and thought that he could make something similar, so it was arranged that they should remain in his room and that his neighbour should come in, when she had time, to clothe them. Johnny thought this a wonderful arrangement and began to save up for these visits the little puzzles of his daily Bible readings, for his intelligence, dormant so long for lack of interest, was now reaching out eagerly towards all that enriched his knowledge of God.

Johnny showed a natural leaning to subjects that could be expressed in pictures and enjoyed the beautifully illustrated books on geography and natural history that Mr. Earnshaw now gladly lent him, but arithmetic was a sore trial to him. He persevered, however, because he was utterly in earnest about his Christianity and he had found in one of his readings the verse, "Whatsoever ye do, do it heartily, as to the Lord, and not unto men." He was happiest in the wood-carving class, where he made such rapid progress that the instructor, laughing, declared that he had "brains in his fingers".

Johnny had one secret from his father—he was making him a pair of carved book-ends for Christmas.

At home he used his new skill to help with the furniture for the dolls' houses for there were certain parts of the work where his small fingers proved more suitable than his father's experienced ones.

In his happiness, Johnny had completely forgotten George Harris. George, however, had not forgotten Johnny. He nursed his hatred, spying on him continually and plotting how to get his revenge without danger to himself. He knew just where Johnny went every day of the week—almost every hour of the day—and decided at last that the time to attack was when Johnny came home from the wood-carving class, for only then was he alone after dark, and one stretch of his way home passed a bombed site where George and his gang could hide until the right moment.

One drizzly evening in early December, George completed his plans, rounded up his gang and laid an ambush. Johnny swung into sight and came towards them, his mind busy on a difficult bit of carving, so that he noticed nothing until there was a soft whistle beside him and at the signal a dozen boys came over the low fence and surrounded him. Johnny recognized George, several of the rougher members of his own old gang and a few from a gang some streets away with whom he had often fought. As he read the festering hatred in George's face, the gloating cruelty of others, his heart sank but his mind worked feverishly.

"No kitten to drown this time?" he taunted. "Twelve to one is just about as cowardly, though!"

George kicked him hard and Johnny winced, but it was no part of his code to shout for help. He had no wish to be called "yellow" or told triumphantly, "So you can't take it, huh?" Instead he put up a silent prayer for help, then hurled himself suddenly against one boy, who reeled aside, and Johnny got his back against a stout timber holding up the fence. He warded off as best he could the blows and kicks that now rained on him, but George drew back for a while and when he next attacked, there was a knife in his hand.

At this moment an office cleaner, coming home from work, rounded a distant corner and saw the boys dimly outlined against a street lamp. As George raised the knife it flashed for an instant and the cleaner, with a muffled squeak of dismay, turned and fled back the way she had come, remembering that she had passed a policeman only a short while ago. He turned at the sound of running feet and she waved and beckoned so frantically that he hurried back towards her.

"It's them Teddy-boys," she shouted, "fighting, and I'm dead sure one of them had a knife—I saw it flash!"

"Where?" he asked, beginning to run.

"Ridley Road, round to the left," she panted. He set off at his best speed; almost immediately the lights of a cruising police car picked him out and the driver accelerated, slowed beside him and he jumped in, giving hasty explanations and directions, dropped off with another man just before they reached the fight and the car stopped a few yards farther on. One lad saw them and shouted,

"Look out, flatties!"

The gang scattered, showing Johnny on the pavement clutching his arm. George and one or two others had vaulted over the fence and were creeping in the darkness across the bombed site, the rest, panicking, ran up or down the road. One man from the police car knelt beside Johnny, the rest, blowing their whistles, scattered after the boys. An approaching motor-cyclist screeched to a stop, calling out,

"What's up, mate? Want any help?" He peered into the shadows. "Why, it's Johnny Connell. You all right, Johnny?"

"Yes, Mr. Carter," replied Johnny cheerfully. The man beside him grunted, working swiftly and skilfully.

"Like your pluck to say so! Severed artery; you might have bled to death on a night like this before anyone noticed you if we hadn't happened along!"

Johnny's voice was weak but quite distinct.

"You didn't 'happen along'—God sent you; I asked Him to send help."

"Well, I'm"—the officer hesitated, then added—"jiggered! Not afraid to show your colours, young 'un!"

"Why should I be?" Johnny sat up. "But I must go home now—Dad will worry."

"That you won't," said the officer firmly. "This is only first aid; you are going to hospital to have some stitches put into that arm of yours and they'll look you over in case anything else needs doing."

"It's all right, Johnny," said Mr. Carter. "I'll let your father know and bring him along to the hospital."

A policeman came up, a boy on each side of him, one sullenly fighting every step of the way, the other weeping with terror and cursing George Harris for getting him into this mess.

"George Harris, eh?" reflected Mr. Carter. "I know him; my boy used to run around with him and he's a real tough customer—probably used the knife. Tell you what, I'll ride round the block and see whether he's trying to sneak out the other side."

He rode off and halted at a corner which showed him two sides of the bombed site; almost immediately three boys climbed over the fence, consulted a moment, then separated. Mr. Carter watched until he was sure which was George then accelerated violently, shot up beside him, and before the lad realized that he had anything to fear flung an arm round him, overpowered him after a brief struggle then returned to Johnny, pushing his machine with one hand and walking George backwards with the other. The police car had returned with two more of the gang, and the driver, looking with contemptuous pity at the still blubbering lad, observed,

"Not much need to worry about the rest; I reckon he'll squeal on the lot!" He turned and looked at George and his captor and began,

"Thank you for your assistance—oh, it's you, Mr. Carter!"

"No offence, mate," replied Mr. Carter quietly. "My boy got what was coming to him—and maybe I did, too. If I'd looked after him a bit better, maybe he wouldn't've got into trouble."

"Anyhow," declared the driver, "you've been of service here; I think you've got the ring-leader. See that bloodstain on his shirt? That'll take a bit of explaining away."

He used his radio and soon the captured boys were at the police station, while Johnny was in hospital immensely interested in being sewn up, and his father was listening open-eyed to his neighbour's story of the fight. Mr. Carter borrowed a friend's motor-cycle with a sidecar and they drove to the hospital to fetch Johnny home, relieved to hear that, although he was badly bruised and the cut was an ugly one, there was no danger in any of his scars.

"He'll soon heal up, don't you worry. As soon as he does, bring him along here and we'll take the stitches out. It might have been much worse!"

Mrs. Rosevear was too sensible to make a great fuss about it, but with Minnie away, Johnny and his father enjoyed many an hour of her quiet help. Johnny really disliked having to attend court and give evidence against the boys who had beaten him up; he even tried to refuse, but Mr. Earnshaw persuaded him that it was his duty.

"You don't want other boys treated as you were, do you? And if these lads are sent to an approved school, they have a good chance of learning to be decent citizens; the discipline may be really good for them."

Johnny saw the force of this, but said as little as possible; he was relieved to find that he did not need to say much as the driver had been right and one boy gave the names of all who had taken part in the fight and told the whole tale of Johnny's rescue of the kitten and how George had been planning revenge ever since. He would not have spoken so freely but for the fact that his father had found work in Birmingham and he knew that he was leaving London for good and would be out of reach of retaliation.

While Johnny had still to be careful in using his arm, Mrs. Rosevear took him with her one evening to see Minnie. He was delighted to find that she was already walking a few steps and hoped to be home very soon, and they spent nearly all the visiting hour in making plans to celebrate her return. Mrs. Rosevear promised that there should be a party on Christmas Day, but they all agreed that if they invited everyone that they would like to invite, they would need a house of at least twice the size!

Chapter 10

JOHNNY WINS HIS BOOK

A FORTNIGHT before Christmas, Mr. Earnshaw took out of the bookcase his volume of *Andersen's Fairy Tales* and opened it at the story of the Tinder Box. When he had explained what a tinder box was, Johnny read, slowly but correctly, the whole of the story. Mr. Earnshaw, who had visited Denmark, explained that the third dog in the story was described as having eyes as big as the Round Tower in Copenhagen, and told him the story of how a king had once driven a coach and horses up the slope inside it leading to the top of the tower.

"What did he do when he got to the top?" inquired Johnny, deeply interested, and was a little disappointed when his teacher confessed that he had never heard. However, they decided that the king had probably left someone else to bring the carriage down and had ridden down himself on one of the horses!

Johnny was scarcely able to speak when Mr. Earnshaw told him that he had fairly earned the book and might take it home as soon as he chose. There was a real battle between his desire to keep the book himself and the more unselfish wish to give it to Minnie for Christmas, but he thought of all he owed to their friendship, and presently he asked Mr.

Earnshaw to keep it for him until he could buy some red paper with holly on it and a piece of red ribbon so as to make it a really Christmassy parcel. Meanwhile he borrowed a pen and wrote in his best writing,

"To Minnie from Johnny with love and best wishes for Christmas."

Mr. Earnshaw had observed and understood the silent battle and the victory, and privately decided to buy for Christmas a book that Johnny could keep for himself—not the same book, for he was quite sure that Minnie would let him read it as often as he wished.

Looking back, it seemed to Mr. Earnshaw that he owed quite a lot to Johnny, who had given him a new interest in life, led him into a wider Christian service and unconsciously broken the shell of selfishness which had begun to form when he lost his wife and had hardened with the death of his only son. In humble thankfulness to God, he made up his mind that not only should there be a Christmas present each for Johnny and Minnie, but he would ask Mr. Venner to name half a dozen of the poorest of his congregation and send them a Christmas parcel apiece. He foresaw much pleasure in arranging with Mr. Venner what each parcel should contain.

Johnny had saved part of his pocket money every week for Christmas. Minnie was to have the book and the dolls' house, the book-ends for his father were nearly ready and he knew that they were the best work he had yet done, but he wanted also to give presents to Mrs. Rosevear and Mr. Earnshaw, and he was surprised to find how many Christmas cards he wanted to send. So many people, he marvelled to himself, had been kind to him, and a card would show them that he remembered and appreciated. Then a new thought came to him; why not a Christmas present for Jesus, Who had given him so much? He spoke to Mr. Venner about it and was delighted to hear that it was the true meaning of the Christmas Tree Service on the following Sunday—that Jesus had said that anything done for any of His people was done for Him.

Johnny had noticed that Mr. Earnshaw liked to use his own Bible and hymn-book at all services and that the hymn-book was now getting a little shabby, so with Mr. Venner's help he bought a new one. For Mrs. Rosevear he bought a bowl of hyacinths just opening their leaves to show their tightly-packed flower-buds, then he bought, stamped, addressed and posted all his Christmas cards. He looked at the money he had left; with the money to come on Saturday there would be just five shillings. Mr. Venner had explained that toys and books from the tree would be sent to children in hospitals and to the very poor who might not have any gifts unless those who love Jesus sent them. Johnny talked to Mrs. Rosevear, looked in every toyshop and bookshop for streets around and at last bought pretty, brightly-coloured picture books, light and easy to hold, for the children in hospital and coloured rubber balls for the poor children for, he thought, both girls and boys can enjoy a ball game and there are so many ways to play with a ball. When he had packed the last parcel he was sure that he had never known such a wonderful Christmas—and this was only the beginning; there was still the Christmas Tree Service, the Carol Service, Christmas Day and Mrs. Rosevear's party, with Minnie back home!

Mrs. Rosevear consulted Mr. Connell before sending out her invitations.

"I want you and Johnny, of course, that's four of us already and my table only holds six. There's my brother and his family, that makes ten—oh, I just don't see how I am to do it."

Mr. Connell looked round the room. There were folding doors between it and Minnie's room at the back and he at once asked whether there was room for Minnie's bed in an upstairs room.

"Yes," decided Mrs. Rosevear, "I think there is; I know you'll help me down with it on Boxing Day."

"*Help* you——!" Mr. Connell was almost speechless with indignation. "A little bit of a bed like that? As if I'd let you lay a finger to it! I could pretty near manage it on my own and Johnny can steer it round the corners. Then my table is bigger than yours; we'll move yours into Minnie's room and put mine in the front room and there's plenty of room for us all."

Mrs. Rosevear looked up hopefully. "Would there be room for more that way? If Mr. Earnshaw would care to come, I don't like to think of him eating his Christmas dinner alone, and the Venners might come to tea."

Mr. Connell was sure it could be done. Chairs? Mrs. Rosevear counted up and could collect a dozen and Mr. Connell promised more if wanted. Then there were plates and dishes. Here Mr. Connell showed some pride.

"My wife was never a smasher—I've still got the best dinner service we had when we were married; twelve of everything, and it's real pretty, and you're welcome to use it, ma'am!"

So the invitations went out, and Mr. and Mrs. Venner were asked if they could drop in at tea-time. Mr. Connell had one more triumphant offer.

"Our firm give us each a turkey at Christmas and it's a beauty, so you don't need to buy that!"

Johnny had a wonderful time with a pot of paste and some rolls of coloured paper, making paper chains, at which he proved as neat-handed as he was at carpentry, and soon both houses were gaily decorated. Mrs. Rosevear's brother sent great branches of holly and some mistletoe from the shop, and with this they wreathed the mirror and some of the pictures, hung sprays from the lights and still had enough left for the centre of each table.

On the day before the Christmas Tree Service

Mr. Connell, passing Mrs. Rosevear's window, glanced in and saw her sitting at her table with dolls spread all over it. He halted, astonished, and she looked up and saw him, laughed at his expression and came to the door to ask whether he could spare her a few minutes. He followed her in and looked at the dolls—dark ones, fair ones, baby dolls, boy and girl dolls and one little angel with silver wings and a star on its forehead. She touched this one gently.

"That's for the top of the tree," she explained happily; "I'm taking that one round tonight."

"Who's having a tree that size?" he asked. "It would have to be big to take that doll."

"The tree in church tomorrow," she explained. "I was wondering if you could help me carry these; it spoils them to crush them together and I shall need four or five carrier bags. Johnny has his own parcel, I know."

Mr. Connell sat down. "You'll have to explain a little. Now you mention it, I remember they gave out something in church last week about a special service, but I thought that if it had been anything to do with me you would have mentioned it."

Mrs. Rosevear looked at him thoughtfully. "There, if I hadn't forgotten that this is your first Christmas at the church. It is one of our favourite services; we all bring gifts, the lights in the church go out leaving just the fairy lights on the tree, then we all take our gifts up, the lighter ones are hung on the tree, the heavier ones are piled beneath it and those who have no other gift put money into a special plate and everything is distributed to hospitals, orphanages and those in need."

Mr. Connell nodded and picked up one of the dolls. "You've been dressing all these for the tree? It must have taken you hours, to say nothing of what you must have spent."

"I love doing it," she protested, "and when it is spread over the whole year, it never gets burdensome."

"I wonder why Johnny didn't tell me? You say he has his parcel ready?"

"Johnny's had a lot on his mind; I expect it has taken him all his time to get his own things ready for Christmas. Besides, you've had your hands full with the dolls' houses."

Mr. Connell shook his head and went through his pockets. "I'll gladly help you carry your dolls, but I'll take a parcel of my own as well," he declared firmly. "If you'll excuse me now, I've just time to buy a few things and next year I'll make my own as you do."

He set off for a toyshop in the main road, thinking as he went, and bought a large jigsaw puzzle, a box of wooden bricks and some pencil boxes stocked with black-lead and coloured pencils. These he took home and studied carefully, showing Johnny how he could glue pictures to plywood and cut them up with a fretsaw, and how easily they could make pencil boxes and wooden bricks, so that by next year they would have enough to bring happiness to many children. He asked about Johnny's gifts and was both pleased and touched by the thoughtfulness that had decided his choice. A tactful question or two showed that Johnny had never even thought that his father knew nothing about the tree.

"Don't you think it *will* be much more fun if we make our own gifts, Johnny?" he asked eagerly and Johnny fully agreed with him.

The next evening, long before service time, they took up their parcels and called next door, where Mrs. Rosevear had carefully packed her dolls into carrier bags and was waiting to show them that Minnie in hospital had not forgotten the tree and had knitted a soft, warm scarf in a pretty shade of blue.

"One of the nurses taught her to knit and someone goes round the wards selling wool, so she was able to choose her own, and she didn't even tell me about it until visiting time today. It is the first one she has missed since she was three, and I didn't speak about it because I thought she might fret over missing it, so you can guess how pleased I was when she showed it to me and asked me to take it tonight."

Since it was all new to the Connells they sat well towards the front of the church so that they might see it all, and when the lights of the church dimmed and went out and the tree sparkled in all the glory of its many fairy lamps, Johnny was by no means the only one to let out a gasp of delight. Slowly, one row at a time, the congregation filed forward, handing their gifts to Mr. or Mrs. Venner or one of the helpers, two of whom, standing on tall ladders, hung gay little dolls and exciting-looking packages until branches bent with their load of gifts. Larger parcels accumulated round the foot of the tree and the two plates on the table were brimming with coins, notes and envelopes. At last all had been up to the front and returned to their places and now the lights came on again to reveal a tree beautified from foot to topmost branch by the loving work of many hands. The hymn of praise and thanksgiving that followed seemed to soar with the joy of realizing that it is indeed more blessed to give than to receive.

Mr. Earnshaw lingered in church after the service to talk to Mr. and Mrs. Venner. Their faces lit up when he explained that he wanted to give a Christmas parcel to the six poorest in the congregation, and Mr. Venner produced a long list of names and addresses and explained that gifts from the tree would go to two local hospitals, an orphanage, a very poor church in the East End of London and some of their own people in special need.

"If you will come round to the small hall at the back, we shall find some of the Men's Fellowship sorting and counting the gifts, and when we have an idea of what is there I can give you a better idea of where your offer can best fit in."

They found a scene of joyful activity; on one table were heaps of dolls, on another, books, elsewhere was a variety of other toys, clothes, shoes, and at a desk the treasurer was counting the money. He looked up as Mr. Venner drew near.

"Thirty-nine pounds, eleven shillings and fourpence," he said; "considering all the other things, it's good for a church this size in a neighbourhood like this." He looked round the room and sighed. "It's a pity there has been so much sickness—we shall have to cut things fine to make it go round."

Mr. Venner laid a hand on his shoulder. "Mr. Earnshaw here wants to take half a dozen people off our list, and he has most generously stipulated that it shall be the six poorest, so perhaps we can do all we hoped."

The treasurer, Mr. Smith, smiled and raised his eyebrows. "The six poorest? That's going to run you into a bit of money! There's Miss Millett, who has spent every penny she has on nursing and then burying her mother, she needs coal as well as a food parcel; there's Mrs. Oliphant, just out of hospital and needing extra food to build her up but with nothing but her widow's pension until she is fit to work again. Then there's Mr. Grattan, whose daughter is at Epsom with mental trouble; he spends every penny he can spare on visiting her and taking little gifts, and I suspect he is starving himself to do it. Are you sure you want more than that?"

Mr. Earnshaw assured him that he did. He thought with shame of his bank balance and the pension he would have when he retired; only a substantial thank-offering would give peace to his conscience, and he noted down names and addresses and asked for advice. Once Mr. Smith had become convinced that Mr. Earnshaw meant literally what he said, he pushed aside his accounts and displayed a really astonishing knowledge of the circumstances, preferences and needs of each of the six. Mr. Earnshaw, taking copious notes, inquired whether it was better to take round his own gifts or to send them through the church.

"Oh, take them round yourself," advised Mr. Smith cordially. "It will mean twice as much to them to feel that you cared enough to think of them as individuals, and you'll find there's a very special happiness in it for you. One of my best friends I first met through taking round a church parcel one year when he'd had a long spell of illness and desperately needed a little help—and I'll never forget the way he and his wife exclaimed over each item in the parcel. One of our church members is the grocer in their street and he'd told Mr. Venner privately the things they bought before Fred's illness and had given up buying since."

So it came about that Mr. Earnshaw, day after day, penetrated into streets in his neighbourhood whose existence he had never suspected, taking with him heavy parcels which seemed to radiate as much joy to giver as to receiver. Poor little Miss Millett, on realizing that not only was her garden shed to be filled to overflowing with good coal at no cost to herself, but she was also to have enough tinned food to fill a whole shelf of her kitchen cupboard and, in addition, a new, thick, fluffy blanket for her bed, laid her thin, work-worn hand on Mr. Earnshaw's strong one and begged him to kneel with her that she might offer thanks to God, Who had not only opened His servant's heart to give but had most wonderfully shown him the very things of which she stood most in need.

Chapter 11

CHRISTMAS PARTY

THREE days before Christmas came the tremendous excitement of Minnie's return home, really walking, though she used a stick to steady herself—but this, she assured them, was not for long.

"There's a room in the hospital where we do exercises and have all sorts of things to help us walk again and a man came and talked to us about keeping on until we were really good at it. He walked and ran, he jumped and skipped, he kicked a football and danced, then he asked us which of his legs was artificial and when we'd all had a guess he showed us that they *both* were, so if he can do it, I know I can!"

"They wanted to keep her in over Christmas," added Mrs. Rosevear, "because they have a lovely time in hospital—a tree, presents, decorated wards, a big Christmas dinner, carols and a Punch and Judy show, but I said, 'You use her bed for some child who won't have much of a time at home; Minnie and I have planned a grand time!'"

"Oh, it would have spoilt everything if Minnie hadn't been at home," agreed Mr. Connell, and Johnny whispered, "'Course it would!"

The next day Johnny helped his father take Mr. Roffen his dolls' house. All the furniture was carefully packed in tissue paper and laid in a big box, which Johnny was just able to manage, while Mr. Connell balanced the house itself on his shoulder; they were both glad they had not far to go. Mr. Roffen welcomed them eagerly and led the way into his bedroom, where he helped them unpack. He had already seen the house more than half completed but he exclaimed over it almost as if he were a child himself, noticing everything and laughing heartily over the tiny cake of soap, the towel rail and the towels in the bathroom. That had been Mrs. Rosevear's idea and she had cut up one of her husband's handkerchiefs to make the dainty towels.

Each piece of furniture had next to be examined, praised and put in its place, but when Johnny produced, from the last wrappings, the three tiny dolls, one in navy trousers and sweater, one in a smart summer dress and jacket and a smaller one in school uniform, Mr. Roffen straightened up and looked at them, his brown eyes aglow with gratitude.

"This is far better than the one we saw in the toy-shop the night I first met you. I can't afford, at the moment, more than the eight pounds I promised you, but you must let me add to that next pay-day—and even then I shall still feel myself in your debt."

But Mr. Connell would not hear of it. "I've had fun making it, mate; I'm glad you're so pleased. And I'll be frank with you—I've learnt a lot making this that has helped me to make Minnie's house even better! You pay me what you first said and I'll be well content. I would like to hear how the little girl likes it, though!"

"You certainly shall," promised Mr. Roffen, "and I think you'll be glad to hear that my wife comes out of hospital tomorrow."

He made them take a big box of crystallized fruits as well as the money, and as they walked home Mr. Connell said happily,

"I'd been wondering whether I could give Mrs. Rosevear a present but I didn't quite know what. She's asked us for the whole of Christmas Day—did I tell you we are even to go to breakfast, so we can see Minnie's face when she first sees her dolls' house? What I've bought is more than enough for Boxing Day, so I'll give her this box of fruits. With eleven asked for dinner and the Venners coming to tea, they won't come amiss!"

On Christmas Eve Mr. Connell brought home the turkey and took it straight in to Mrs. Rosevear, who gazed in consternation.

"Shall I be able to get it in the oven, do you think?"

They tried it and found that it would just go in but would certainly leave no room for anything else. Mr. Connell suggested,

"If you can manage to run between, you could use our oven as well."

"Oh, yes; the sausages and roast potatoes can do in there and the boiled potatoes and sprouts on top and that will leave my top clear for the bread sauce, pudding and custard."

Mr. Connell and Johnny moved Minnie's bed upstairs, and as soon as she was in it they brought over the dolls' house, which was mounted on little casters so that it could turn easily to show either back or front. Johnny put in the furniture and Mrs. Rosevear settled the little Dutch dolls in the drawing-room, then Johnny and his father brought over their big table and put it in the front room, carefully washed and carried over the dinner service and did what they could to make all ready.

When they went home, they found that there had been a late postal delivery and Johnny picked up a large envelope with his own name on it. He was delighted to find not only a card from Rosemary and Marigold, but a note to say that their father was bringing them to London on Boxing Day to visit some cousins and they had made him promise to come up extra early so that they could see Johnny and Minnie.

"Of course," explained Johnny, "they are coming to see Minnie really; I only met them that once but Minnie was with them a whole fortnight—but isn't it nice that they want to see me, too! That's another thing to look forward to! Don't we have grand times now, Dad?"

Mr. Connell agreed, and looked on with some pride as Johnny added this card, a lovely sea picture with a sailing ship, to the already large display on the sideboard, more than half of which were from people they had met since the Rosevears came to live next door, and he thought, as he had done many times recently, how much he and Johnny owed to their friendship.

Usually Johnny was asleep almost as soon as he lay down but tonight he was too excited to sleep at once; he thought about his letter, his day at the seaside and how it had led to the wood-carving classes; that led on to the book-ends he had made for his father, and he wondered how they would be received. Then he thought of all he owed Mr. Earnshaw and was glad he was coming to the party tomorrow; from there his thoughts drifted to the other guests. He stopped there for a very earnest thanksgiving, and that brought peace to the confusion of his thoughts, but just as he was drifting off to sleep one more thought came. When he put all the things in Minnie's dolls' house he had had a good look at the Dutch dolls and had noticed that they were not exactly like the ones his father had made for Rose Roffen. Those three, although made to the same plan, were somehow different, and it came to him now what the difference was. The father doll, decidedly the biggest of the three, was just a tiny bit like his own father, while the plump, comfortable mother doll with her black hair, rosy cheeks and blue eyes, was like—was like—yes, that was it! Like Mrs. Rosevear!

In spite of this unusual wakefulness, Johnny woke before his usual time on Christmas Day and crept out to the kitchen for a very special scrubbing so that no one might find on him a speck of dirt or so much as a hair out of place; he wanted to do honour to his friends.

Very soon his father was up and they called a Merry Christmas to each other. Mr. Connell added with a twinkle,

"If you was to look in the coal-shed, Johnny, you might find something that would interest you!"

"The coal-shed?" repeated Johnny, bewildered, and he went into the garden trying hard to think what could be there. When he found a neat, strong bicycle, just the right size for him, he could only come back, put his arms round his father and say over and over again, "Oh, Dad!"

Presently, however, he brought out his own gift and Mr. Connell marvelled over the neat construction and the really pretty carving of leaves and flowers, and had to put them up on the sideboard and gather together his few books to stand between them. He could quite honestly assure Johnny that the gift was a real pleasure to him, for not only had it obviously taken many hours of work, but it showed real talent and gave promise for the future.

They were soon ready for next door, where Minnie had been at her wits' end to find out why she must not go into the front room until they came. Now, however, Mrs. Rosevear threw open the door and Minnie followed the visitors into the room and caught her first sight of her present. She ran forward to look and touch, flushed with pleasure and scarcely able to believe that it was for her.

"See there!" triumphed her mother. "She ran, and without her stick!"

"Oh, it's beautiful! It's just the nicest dolls' house I've ever seen! Did you make it? And is it really for me?"

"I had a lot of help from Johnny," Mr. Connell told her. "We made it together and every little bit of it was for you!"

He showed her how to open the front, how to turn it round and open the back, and she kept making fresh discoveries and exclaiming over each one, thanking them both over and over again. Then Johnny gave her the book and took the bowl of hyacinths which his father had carried for him, wrapped in tissue paper, and these, too, gave great pleasure, and when Mr. Connell offered his gift, Mrs. Rosevear, her eyes bright with unshed tears, remarked,

"Do you know, I had dreaded this first Christmas after my husband's death and thought it would be so unhappy, but you've been so kind and good and gone to so much trouble that I know it's going to be a wonderful day."

Now she gently called Minnie away from her treasures and said,

"Don't you think it's time we brought out our parcels, my chick?"

Minnie dimpled merrily and slipped out of the room, returning almost at once with four gay-looking parcels, two large and two small. Mr. Connell opened his small parcel first and found six handkerchiefs, each with his initials, F.C., and a card, "With every good wish for Christmas from your friend Annie Rosevear."

He looked up, gratitude and bewilderment in his face, and could not help asking as he thanked her how she had found out his first initial. She admitted that she had remembered it after reading in the local paper an account of his wife's death. He now turned to his other parcel, since Johnny was spinning out the excitement by refusing to open either of his until he had seen his father's gifts. The second was from Minnie, a pictorial calendar with a text for every day of the year. He was so pleased with this that he put his arm round her and kissed her, to which she responded heartily, for she had taken a great liking to him.

Now Johnny opened his gifts. Again the smaller parcel was from Mrs. Rosevear and Johnny exclaimed delightedly over a penknife with four strong blades. Minnie watched with some anxiety as he turned to the last parcel, for this was her own idea, although her mother had approved and carried it out for her. A plain tin box held a dozen carefully chosen pans of water-colour and three good-quality brushes, and Johnny, eyes alight, cried,

"Oh, Minnie, how *did* you guess?"

This, she felt, was her best thanks—better than anything he said afterwards—for it revealed that he had been wishing for paints. He had even meant to begin saving up for some when Christmas was over.

And now Mrs. Rosevear looked at the clock and

laughed. "What a good thing I didn't arrange to put breakfast on the table the minute you came! It would all be spoilt by now! Minnie doesn't feel Christmas is complete unless she has stewed turkey giblets for breakfast; does anyone else like them?"

"I do," admitted Johnny, but Mr. Connell hesitated and when she suggested scrambled eggs and mushrooms on toast confessed that for him it would be much more of a treat. After breakfast all helped to clear and wash up, then began a sort of disciplined rush. Mrs. Rosevear was an excellent organizer and seemed to know the exact moment that everything should be done, so that when her other guests came she had time for greetings and chat, the tables were set and the food ready to dish up. Mr. Earnshaw had found a series of books about a mission hospital in Africa, so simple that he knew Minnie could enjoy them yet so fascinating that he had himself sat up late on two successive nights to finish reading them before giving them away. He gave half the series to Minnie and the rest to Johnny, suggesting that they should read them together. He had also brought a two-pound box of chocolates, though he wondered, when he saw what Mrs. Rosevear had provided, whether anyone would be able to touch them! However, six of those present were children, and he was amazed to see them getting through roast turkey and all its trimmings and still prepared to tackle Christmas pudding and custard. Mrs. Rosevear warned them that there were silver charms in the pudding and there was general laughter when Johnny found a sixpence, Mr. Earnshaw a thimble, and Mrs. Rosevear a ring!

There were hot mince pies, too, and fruit, nuts, chocolates and marzipan until even the children admitted that they could eat no more, then they were set free and made with one accord for the dolls' house while their elders cleared away and washed up. It was really astonishing the fun they had with the house, for first they had to explore it from the roof downwards, then it must all be shown to the grown-up members of the party, and they had hardly finished that before Mr. and Mrs. Venner arrived and admired it and Mr. Venner asked Mr. Connell whether he would make two or three more by the following Christmas for an orphanage and one or two children's hospitals.

"If Johnny will help me, I should like to do it. When you've spent weeks on a big job like this you kind of miss it when it's finished."

They played some of the quieter games for, with so many in the two rooms, there was no space for boisterous play, then they sang Christmas carols together and very soon Mr. Venner was suggesting that both Mrs. Rosevear and Mr. Connell should join the church choir.

It was not long after tea before little Valerie, who was only five, dropped off to sleep, and Mr. Robson decided to take his family home before too much excitement made the children fretful.

That left only seven, and when Minnie and Johnny said they would like to sit quietly and look at their new books, the others settled down to talk. One after another spoke of how much happier the day had been than they could possibly have hoped, and quite simply and naturally Mr. Venner gathered it all up into a prayer of praise and thanskgiving to God. So much had happened that they could not have foreseen a year ago, and although there had been trouble and sorrow they had been so wonderfully led through and helped that when Mr. Venner quoted,

> "All things work together for good unto them that love God,"

Mr. Connell had to reply,

"That's it in a nutshell, sir."

Johnny said something about Alfie Carter and that prompted Mr. Venner to mention something he had in mind.

"All these young gangsters in the neighbourhood—it's time we did something about them. I didn't know Johnny when he was a gang leader, but here he is as proof that being in a gang doesn't mean that you are vicious and worthless; as soon as Johnny felt that somebody loved him and took an interest in him, he began to change and to find that there was pleasure in doing right that appealed to him more than getting into mischief. I am certain that that is the root of the trouble in most cases; divided homes—you won't mind my being frank, Mr. Connell—and too little to do. Alfie Carter could help protect Minnie from a bully, some of Johnny's gang were willing to fight to save a kitten's life—there *is* good in all of them.

"Now Johnny here could give us the names of boys whom we might be able to help, and we could tackle them as soon as we work out some plan, and by the time the rougher ones are set free we should have a nucleus to go out after them, too, particularly if the discipline they have been through has done them good and given them any desire to be different."

"What do you suggest, sir?" asked Mr. Connell. "I'd be willing to do what I could; I feel as if I—well, I owe that."

"There's a family just down the road," put in Mrs. Rosevear eagerly. "The father knocks them about when he's in drink and the mother, with eight to look after, is the sort who lets them do as they like till they go too far, then hits them and screams at them—they none of them know where they are and mostly they're out in the streets to keep out of the way. How would it be if I tried to make friends with them?"

"That would be a beginning," agreed Mr. Venner, "but I want to face the fact that the gang spirit is natural in a boy, and get them together under better leadership to do something that will work off steam and at the same time really interest them."

"If we only had somewhere we could all meet,"

suggested Johnny, who had been listening, "somewhere pretty big where we could have a lot of things going on and then ask them in two or three at a time to see what we are doing and see if they like it." He broke off and thought for a moment or two, but Mr. Venner, feeling that more was to follow, waited in expectant silence. Johnny went on slowly, almost as if thinking aloud.

"There's Keith Morton at our wood-carving class; we were talking after my arm was cut and he said he had no time for this gangster stuff. One day a week he's at wood-carving, one day it's table tennis in winter and cricket in summer, one day he goes swimming—he's awfully good at that—wins medals and cups and things—one day he stays at home and looks after his brothers and sisters while his parents have an evening out, one day he goes to a gymnasium. Saturday, if it's fine, he and two of his brothers go cycling in the country, and Sunday his Mum and Dad are home all day and they all tell about everything they've done all through the week. He says there's no time for getting into mischief."

Mr. Venner nodded thoughtfully; it agreed so well with his own ideas, and now he told them,

"I have the promise of that bombed site where George Harris and his gang hid, Johnny, if I can raise enough money to build a hall. It's not too far from the church—I could wish it were nearer, but there is nothing suitable—and if we can interest enough people and build and equip it, we may do something to win them over. Meanwhile, as Mrs. Rosevear says, let's make friends with them."

"That's what began it all with me," Johnny remembered, "just that Mrs. Rosevear was friendly. I didn't seem to matter to anyone before that." Then, knowing that he had hurt his father, he added quickly, "But we're going to forget all that, now that we've learnt better, eh, Dad?"

"No, son," replied Mr. Connell soberly. "We'll forget the bitterness of it but we're going to remember everything that gives us a pointer to the way to help others. That's right, isn't it, sir?"

"The great thing," said Mr. Venner, flashing a smile at them, "is that God has said He will forget! 'Their sins and their iniquities will I remember no more'."

"It's a comforting thought, and more than I feel I deserve. Then it's agreed that we try for a church hall? I shall want to give—say two bob a week until it's built—as a sort of thank-offering for the difference in me and Johnny. Could I have a box and drop in what I can afford week by week?"

Then it was time to say good-bye. Mrs. Rosevear, looking rather ruefully at the food that had *not* been eaten, tried to persuade them to have a little more before leaving, but without success.

Mr. Connell suggested that Mrs. Rosevear should put Minnie to bed while he cleared up; Johnny could put himself to bed and he would stay a while and help wash up. Mrs. Rosevear protested at first, but admitted that it would be a help, so the youngsters rather reluctantly came to the end of their wonderful day. Mr. Connell washed while his neighbour wiped and at first they had plenty to say, but soon Mr. Connell became silent and thoughtful. Mrs. Rosevear looked at him several times and at last said,

"You're tired yourself; leave me to finish these—you've done so much already and I don't know how to thank you for it all."

"I'm not a bit tired," he assured her, "just thinking; it's been on my mind for some time now."

"If anything's troubling you, would you care to tell me? You know the saying—a trouble shared——"

"Oh, it isn't a trouble! I don't quite know how to tell you—or whether you'd care to hear it, come to that."

"I'd care to hear anything that you'd care to tell me."

"Well, then—I was thinking it would be—mighty fine"—he faltered—"if Johnny had a mother and if Minnie had a father."

Mrs. Rosevear gasped. "Well, really!" she said. "Are you—are you trying to——"

"Yes, I am," he replied. "I don't find it easy, seeing you know what I was only such a short time ago, but I think you know that *that's* all done with, for I found that what I couldn't do for myself, Jesus Christ can do for me. I haven't the love to offer that I gave my first wife, but I'm not sure I'd want to if

I could, and I rather think that the way I feel about you is more lasting, and I could be a good father to Minnie for I love her already and she seems to love me."

"Well," mused Mrs. Rosevear, "I tell you frankly you've taken me by surprise. I had a good husband and I never thought to marry again."

"I can see you're not going to say yes at once and I suppose I can hardly expect it, but don't say no at once either. I'm willing to wait if you'll give me even a hope that some day you might say yes."

"Then say no more about it until a year from the day your wife died, and if you're still of the same mind then, and still going on steadily as a Christian, I'm not saying but it might be yes. I couldn't have imagined it possible when I first met you, but considering what God has already made of you in these few months, I believe I may yet find you such as I could promise to love, honour and obey."

"Thank you—Annie," he ventured. She flushed, smiled and took up the last cup, dried it with extra care and hung it on its hook. Mr. Connell, suddenly shy, cleaned the bowl and wiped his hands.

"I'll be going now," he said, "and thank you for everything. It's been a wonderful day."

She saw him to the door and, quite unconsciously, stood beneath the spray of mistletoe hanging from the hall light. A sudden twinkle came into his eyes as he noticed it.

"By your leave, ma'am!" he said, kissing her, and

before she could say a word he had quietly shut the door behind him and stepped, chuckling, over to his own front door. Mrs. Rosevear frowned, smiled and shook her head.

"I can see," she thought, "that I shan't have much chance to say no. I didn't think, when Johnny talked of marrying Minnie, bless him, that I might marry his Daddy instead!"